BURN ME

AN IMMORTAL VICES
AND VIRTUES NOVEL

K.A. KNIGHT

KENDRA MORENO

Burn Me (Immortal Vices and Virtues Book Ten).

Written by K.A. Knight & Kendra Moreno
Edited By Jess from Elemental Editing and Proofreading.
Formatted by The Nutty Formatter.
Cover by Yocla Designs.

CHAPTER 1
ROUX

As I soar high above Celestia, my copper and blonde streaked hair floats past me on the wind as I glide through the clouds, the sun shining down on my white feathered wings. My runes burn bright with my power, echoed across my tan skin and pale wings. I feel the strength in my body, my muscles tensing as I turn and swoop lower over my homeland—muscles I have honed over my many years as a descendant of seraphim, those who rule us. All who are born of their blood are archangels, and they protect our lands and our people.

They are warriors, just like me.

Cherubim are just trouble, while dominions rule over the warriors. The only other class of angels above us archangels are virtues, those born with control over the elements. There are many below us, like half-breeds and those born with lesser power, but the archangels? We are the most important, if I do say so myself.

But everyone has a place in Celestia.

As always, my breath catches in my lungs as I pass through the clouds and my world comes into focus, shining brightly with our angelic powers.

My eyes go to the palace of angels first, or the Palace of Pia, which reaches up toward the heavens. The white and gold architecture is so stunning, I almost wept the first time I saw it from above. The spires proudly display our golden sun flag, the huge, sprawling mass of the structure inhabited by our leader. Everyone else lives throughout the city and the other areas across the islands.

From below, Celestia only looks like a giant rock with other rocks surrounding it, but from above, you see the beauty and size of our world. The palace sits in the middle of the main part of our lands, with gardens and greenery surrounding it. Houses and shops stretch out to the edges, while training areas, schools, and additional housing are located on the adjacent rocks, or islands as we call them, which you have to fly to.

There are advantages to wings, after all.

Everything on our islands is done in the same brilliant white and gold, so when the sun hits it, reflecting off the glimmering architecture, my eyes almost water as I swoop lower and lower. I wave and smile at others in greetings as I slow and glide past the edges of our world, seeing the one underneath.

Deeper below Celestia is a wasteland. The rugged terrain sits between us and the demons, which are fiery beings that hide under the ruined crust of the Earth. For a moment, sadness washes over me. The desert wasteland stretches as far as the eye can see. Nothing green or good is left, thanks to the battles that have taken place there over the years.

It's unlike Celestia. Our world floats high in the clouds. Angels train in the sky, children learn to fly by leaping off the islands, and archangels like me learn to fight while jumping between treacherous stones. Some simply enjoy the sun since we're so close to it.

There is nothing more perfect than our world, I think idly as I land on the edge of a clearing near the training house for archangels. We inhabit the island to the very right—the higher in rank we are, the better housing we get.

Since I was on patrol, I need to report back to let them know I didn't see any demons or traps. After all, the demons are our enemies. We have been at war with them for centuries, always fighting and warring.

It's a tale as old as time—good versus evil.

They are brutal killing machines with no conscience, hence why they live below the crust of the world, burning for their sins as they should.

Flipping my hair over my shoulder, I tuck my wings in, as is polite, and stride through the fighting masses. Angel sticks and glowing swords ring out as they clash with shouts of encouragement following. The familiar sounds make me smile, and I ache to join in, to prove myself and put myself to the test.

I have only been granted the archangel rank for a little over eighty sun rotations now, and after training, I was put on patrol. I hope, as I prove myself, I can work my way up. I would love to see more of our world and of Earth through the portal. I have been a few times—sometimes when I shouldn't—and it is an incredible place filled with so many species and types of people.

The rules are not the same there, and for a moment, I long for that freedom before Ajop, the leader of the training school, spots me and beckons me over, stilling all other thoughts.

He stands with his thick arms crossed over his chest, his runes glowing softly under his pale skin in a way that makes me envious. His golden hair is pushed back from his perfect angelic face, and his gold eyes flash as he watches my approach. No emotions show on the beautiful, stoic leader's face.

"Report," he orders when I get closer, using the only tone of voice I've ever heard from him.

I often wonder how old he is. Rumors state that he's been a warrior since before many others were born.

I duck my head and bring my hand to my chest, as is customary when speaking to an elder. "No signs of any disturbances to the east. I flew as far as the guyster—"

"You should not have done that," he snaps, the vibration in his tone displaying his displeasure. "You must be able to follow orders to be a good warrior, Roux."

"I apologize, Commander Ajop," I reply immediately, wincing at my stupidity. I shouldn't have admitted to going farther than I was ordered. "I simply wish to be of use to our people."

"Then do as you are told, and you will."

"I was simply thinking—"

"We are not to think. We are to follow orders. Is that understood?" His voice is lower now, and the fighting near us has stopped as everyone watches me be disciplined for my disobedience.

"Yes, Commander," I murmur sincerely. "I will clean out the stalls as punishment."

"And you will visit the church and offer your apologies to the divine for being so incompetent," he orders.

"Of course, Commander." I duck my head farther, hiding the sadness in my gaze.

I only wish to help. I wish they could see that and recognize that I am capable of so much more. If they only let me, I could be everything they need in this war against the demons, but for now, I scurry away, ignoring the laughter of the other archangels as I head to my punishment.

Along the way, I spot Rosa struggling with the wagon holding a new shipment of spears and swords from the blacksmith. Without thought, I hurry closer and take the other handle, helping her haul the cumbersome load. The weight is substantial and makes sweat bead on my brow, and I wonder how she carried it all this way herself.

"Thank you, Roux," she says, peering at me with her bright green eyes. She's smaller than my five-eight height, and her curves are hidden beneath her cream and gold cloak, like her master blacksmith insists. She's beautiful, just as all angels are, with her fiery red hair and perfect pale skin. The red hue of her hair has always gotten her in trouble, though, and it means a lot of people stay away from her. Rumor has it she was born from demon fire.

It's stupid, and Rosa is a lovely woman. She doesn't deserve their slander.

"You are too kind," she murmurs.

"Don't be silly. No one would walk past and leave you struggling," I reply with a huff.

"You are too naïve," she replies before laughing. "They would in order to avoid being infected by demon fire."

I groan at that as we reach the back of the school and drop the wagon. "They are foolish." I wince then and look around. If anyone heard, I would be punished harsher.

"And they take your kindness for granted," Rosa states, squeezing my hand. "Now go along with whatever you were doing. I do not want to taint your reputation."

"You never could, but I do have things to do. See you later." I wave to her then hurry to the church on the next island over to beg for my forgiveness.

I hope that Rosa is wrong and that I am not naïve or overly kind. One day, I want to be the incredible warrior and leader I've always wanted to be.

One day, I tell myself.

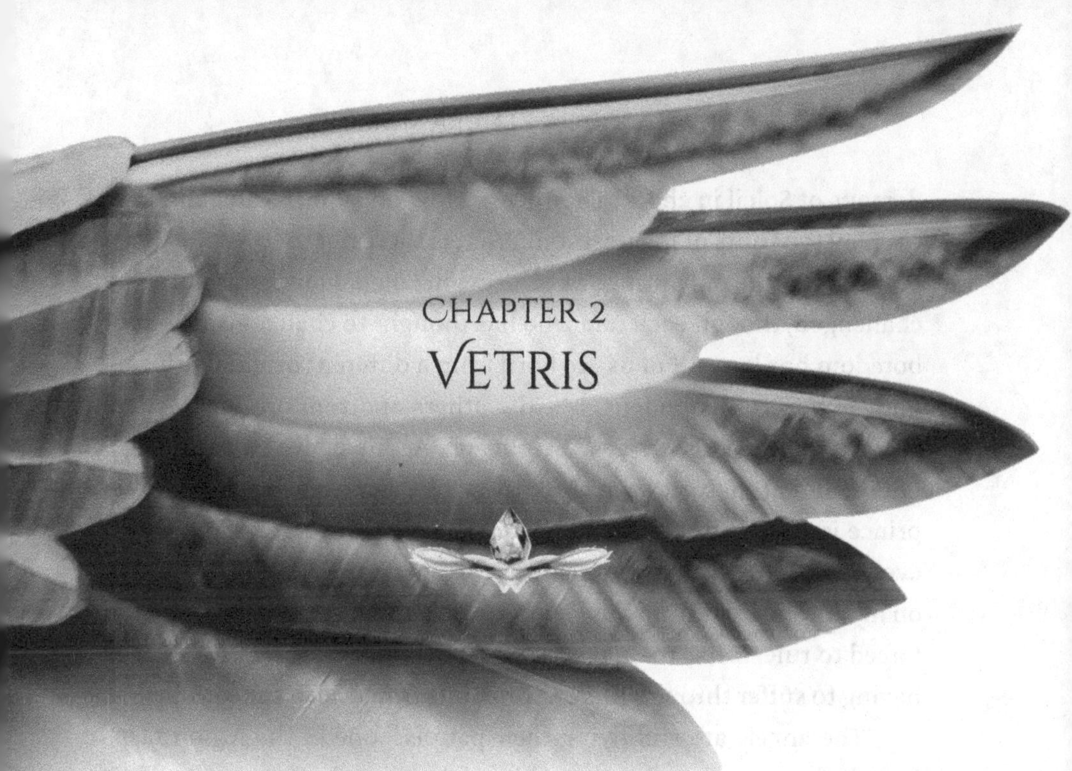

CHAPTER 2
VETRIS

I watch in amusement as the mischief demons run around the throne room. Their penchant for trouble causes the incubi and succubi lounging in the space to groan in frustration. I don't mind the heathens myself, feeling far more amused than annoyed, but this is Soleil, after all.

What is the use of a demonic realm if not for debauchery?

Down here, the world is dark and humid, and the stone walls sweat with the moisture in the air. If I wasn't crown prince, it would be uncomfortable. As it is, the hellfire is my home. It licks at my boots as I sit on my throne with my legs spread wide, caressing me like a familiar friend. When needed, it will climb along my arms and alert anyone near that death flirts at their door.

The perks of being the current reigning crown prince.

Every year, one of the seven princes and princesses is chosen to rule Soleil. This year, the task has been passed to me. As a child of Asmodeus, I take the assignment seriously—so seriously, there is an orgy every week for those who wish to partake. If they don't, they get to watch the show. Lust is a heady drug, and it helps keep the demons of Soleil in check. They get to blow off some steam, and I get to enjoy the fruits of my position. What is there not to love?

I am not the only prince or princess in Soleil, however, so I can be challenged, though each one who has thought to challenge me out of boredom has lost. All of us are born from a different original prince. I may be born of Asmodeus, but the others are from original leaders such as Lilith, Lucifer, and Belphegor. At birth, we're assigned a house, and at maturity, we enter the ranks. Every year, a new crown prince is chosen by the scroll. I don't know how it works, only that every so often, my name appears as the next crown prince. Now, I sit on my throne built from angel bones and suffer the boredom of being forced to rule. It has its perks, but it also has its drawbacks—such as having to suffer through more complaints from those beneath me.

"The angels are still flying their patrols," one of the legion rasps from before me. I don't know this one's name, but even if I did, it wouldn't matter. The legion is a single unit better referred to as a group than individuals. Their only purpose is to scout and to serve, and during war, their task turns to swarming. "They grow bolder each day. My brother was stabbed by an archangel just the other day. I fear—"

"I don't care." I sigh, tapping my finger against the throne. "A loss of a single legion is hardly cause for worry."

The legion's face twists with malice. "That legion was my brother."

"As are all legion." I lean forward. "Would you like to join the one who feeds the hellfire, miscreant?"

For a second, I think he'll challenge me and make things interesting. If he has the courage to do such a thing, I might even let him fight. Bravery is not only entertaining, but it's also valuable. A brave legion can change the tides of war. This one looks like all the others—upturned mouth, fangs peeking over its lip, large ears tilted down into points, large head filled with rambunctious war cries, and short stature. There are discrepancies between the legion, but for the most part, they all look the same. Perhaps this one will surprise me, but in the end, he slowly shakes his head and bows low, offering his submission.

I scowl in disgust. "Then get out of my sight. Next time you come to report something, make sure it's actual news. I tire of these foolish complaints."

The legion scuttles off with fear in his eyes. He should fear me. I've been known to lose my cool and decimate demons who get in my way. In a war, I can't be so callous so often, so I keep my cool despite the fire climbing up my legs.

"The legion is correct," Manon, a succubus, says once the demon is gone. She lies on a chaise to my right, her breasts out for all to partake of. "The angels will attack soon. I've had a feeling."

"Oh, you've had a feeling?" I mock, rolling my eyes. "Did you feel it in your nipples? Do they tingle in warning?"

She scowls. "Fuck you, Vetris. It's a sixth sense."

I shouldn't allow the lack of formality, but I've never been one to punish someone for using my name. Besides, she isn't disrespecting me. If I stood up, she'd slide to the floor and prostrate herself before me like a needy little succubus should, but I have no desire for such games today. Instead, the constant warnings of the angels' movement are getting to my head and annoying me.

"Everyone out," I growl, rubbing my temples as a headache starts to grow.

Quickly, the succubi, incubi, and horde of mischief demons tumble over each other to clear my throne room. Only Manon lingers at the door.

"Do you need anything, My Most Terrible Lord?" she asks, her lips pouting out in a way that tells me she'll do anything. I'm not amused. Manon has always been attractive, but her red skin and curling horns don't delight me in the way it might have a hundred years ago. I have no desire for the demon before me. Her black wings drape around her like a robe right now, looking more bat-like than mine, which are covered in feathers. Of course, she can shapeshift into whatever I'd like, but that hardly holds the same appeal as actually fucking whom I want. I'd learned that long ago.

In lieu of answering, I wave my hand at her to go, and the door closes behind her, leaving me mostly alone in the throne room. The hellfire never leaves, nor do the shadows. They cling to me as the reigning prince, both a curse and a blessing. I hate them. Every time I'm chosen, I loathe the feeling of the flames climbing along my flesh to designate my reign. I also despise how they are cold to the touch, leaving me more chilled than hot. Mostly, I despise that I have to suffer the stupid demons who keep warning of impending doom. The angels wouldn't be so foolish to attack Soleil again. They have their stupid city in the sky, Celestia, where they sit like pretty, untouchable birds. They have no reason to come back down to Soleil and start another war. The last one left the wasteland between us, desecrated land where nothing grows. Even standing there makes me sad. To leave such ruination...

But the angels asked for such.

Though we are no longer actively at war, the angels control the skies and we control the area beneath Earth's surface. We do not mix. We stay in our designated areas and make sure the other does the same.

The urge to put the angels in their place is strong. All demons would like to pluck their feathers one by one from their wings, hold the golden, glittery things up to hellfire, and watch them burn to ash. Those wings are signs of their purity and goodness.

It's bullshit.

Nothing could be further from the truth.

Just as their wings are pure and bright, our wings are dark and inky. I spread my own wings at my back, letting them touch each side of the massive throne room, my feathers stroking the stone. The very tips fade from back to red, as if they have been dipped in the blood of my enemies. I yearn to fly, to spread them in the open air, but I'd risk too much as a crown prince if I went up to the wasteland and took flight. A crown prince moving in such a way is a declaration of war, and although a war would ease the boredom, countless lives would perish. I'd rather my reign wasn't affiliated with something like that. My reign should consist of nothing but sex and drunken debauchery.

That's how it always is.

The hellfire to my right flickers and draws my attention, highlighting the hellhound that prances there. The great beasts are bothersome at the worst of times, but as the crown prince, I should be able to control them and speak to them.

I pat my thigh and whistle, my brow lowered in animosity. It's an order, one that shouldn't be ignored. The hellhound glances up at the whistle, sees I'm calling, and goes right back to what it was doing.

As they always do.

Scowling, I snap my wings closed in anger and cross my arms. "Fucking useless beasts," I growl, and then I storm from the throne room, tiring of the scenery. I need some air, some space.

Some freedom.

There's no such thing for the crown prince however.

CHAPTER 3
ROUX

After cleaning every stall of the pegasi us archangels use, I spend hours begging for forgiveness on the floor of the church. My pleas for the divine echo around me despite the other angels present. The divine does not answer, of course, but I feel better all the same.

I have always been too impulsive and free thinking. I think our people assumed that when I was finally selected to be an archangel, it would control me. I guess some angels are just not as easy to mold. Do not get me wrong, I will gladly follow orders and protect and respect our people, but little things.... That can't be so bad, right? Like flying when we are supposed to be grounded, or getting drunk and committing sins of the flesh before mating.

The job still gets done, so I do not see the issue.

Sighing, I swing my legs back and forth on the edge of the island, backlit by the church filled for the divine's service. I should be there, showing my respect and love for our god, but here I am, feeling sorry for myself.

Which do I choose? The glittering throng behind me, or the open sky before me?

My choice is stolen when a noise reaches me on the wind. I leap to my feet, worried it could be an attack. Those tricky demons love the dark, and if they were to attack, it would be under the cloak of nightfall, their flaming eyes their only tell. Not wanting to be the angel who lets demons slip past, I leap from the island and into the night in search of the sound.

The noise echoes in the night once more. Frowning, I fly closer and closer to the wasteland below before finally landing silently. Bringing my wings in, I cock my head and close my eyes as I once again search for the sound. The heat of the ground underneath almost burns my feet, but instead I focus on the sounds.

The shifting rocks, the wind, and below it all?

Voices.

Leaping into the air, I take off in their direction before landing once more in a rocky outcropping above where the voices are originating. At first, I see nothing, and I wonder if I have finally gone mad. It happens, usually with age, but I've always been an early bloomer.

Suddenly, from behind two large rocks, the beings responsible for the voices emerge. Shock courses through me, and I freeze in the shade of the outcropping concealing me from them. My wings tuck in tight, and I keep my powers contained so I do not glow and give myself away.

My heart thrums in confusion and wariness, because before me is an angel and a demon.

They are not attacking one another, but talking, their heads almost bent together, and more emerge from the rocks. Neither of the species is attacking or fighting. No, they almost seem to be... working together.

It cannot be. We are sworn enemies. Wars have been fought for years over our animosity.

Yet the evidence is undeniable. Something changes between them, and the angels speak in low registers to the grinning demons. It is... They are... They are working together and breaking every covenant of our people.

The archangels must not know. Our leaders must not know.

I have to tell them, I realize. I have to make them aware.

This is bad. This is unbelievably bad.

I wait for them to disappear. The angels take flight without even looking around, which is foolish, and the demons chuckle as they watch them go, mocking them before sinking back into the holes in the ground.

Not wanting to be caught lingering, I push myself into the sky, flying as hard and as fast back to Celestia as I can. I land before the palace and hurry inside, ignoring the calls and looks, but I'm stopped before the stairs.

"Archangel, what are you doing?" a palace guard snaps.

"Please, I must speak with the seraphim!" I plead, knowing I must look half mad. "It's an emergency."

Frowning, he looks me over before nodding. "I shall put in the call. Please wait here."

I do as I am told, fidgeting, pacing, and worrying on my lip when a voice snaps me to attention.

"Archangel, what is the meaning of this?"

I drop to my knees before one of our great leaders, one of the oldest and most powerful of our kind—Rael. "Your greatness," I begin as he stops before me.

"They said it was an emergency. Why do I see only one lowly archangel instead of our flock?" His voice is angry, and I wince.

"I am sorry. I could not wait to inform my superior. It was imperative I told you what I saw."

He harrumphs. "Ah, Ajop, there you are. Is this one of yours?" Rael calls.

I flinch but do not raise my head.

"Unfortunately so. What is the meaning of this, Roux?" Ajop demands, now standing next to Rael.

"I saw angels and demons together in the wasteland," I tell them hurriedly.

"And why were you on Earth without orders? Why were you

flying at night when not on patrol?" Rael's voice booms.

I jerk my head down, squeezing my wings shut.

"I heard a noise, and I was worried about an attack. Please, your divine greatness, you must let me—"

"You disobeyed your orders. You could have started a war!"

"They were working together!" I surge to my feet. "They were not attacking, they were together."

I pant, glancing between them. I know they could have my wings for the disrespect, but they must know how serious I am. Rael's eyes narrow on me, and he looks to Ajop. They seem to share some sort of silent communication before he nods at me.

"I see. That is not what I heard," Rael begins silkily.

"Your greatness?" I ask, confused.

"I have received reports that you are working with the demons on Earth and stole the orb."

"Orb?" I repeat as they surround me, something worrying prickling deep within.

"The orb, child! It is missing, and you... you admitted to being on Earth," he hisses.

"No, wait, I was there to—"

"You are a thief. You did not see angels and demons together. You know you were spotted stealing the orb and tried to cover yourself."

"I-I didn't—"

"Guards, take the traitor to the cells. She will be sentenced before all tomorrow."

Before I can even protest my innocence, I am surrounded, my wings are chained, and my hands are bound together, then I am dragged from the palace. My eyes stay on our leaders as I am taken away. In their gazes, I see a smug relief, and the truth makes me sag in defeat.

They know about the meeting, and worst of all, they have set me up.

Oh heaven, I'm naïve.

How am I going to get out of this one?

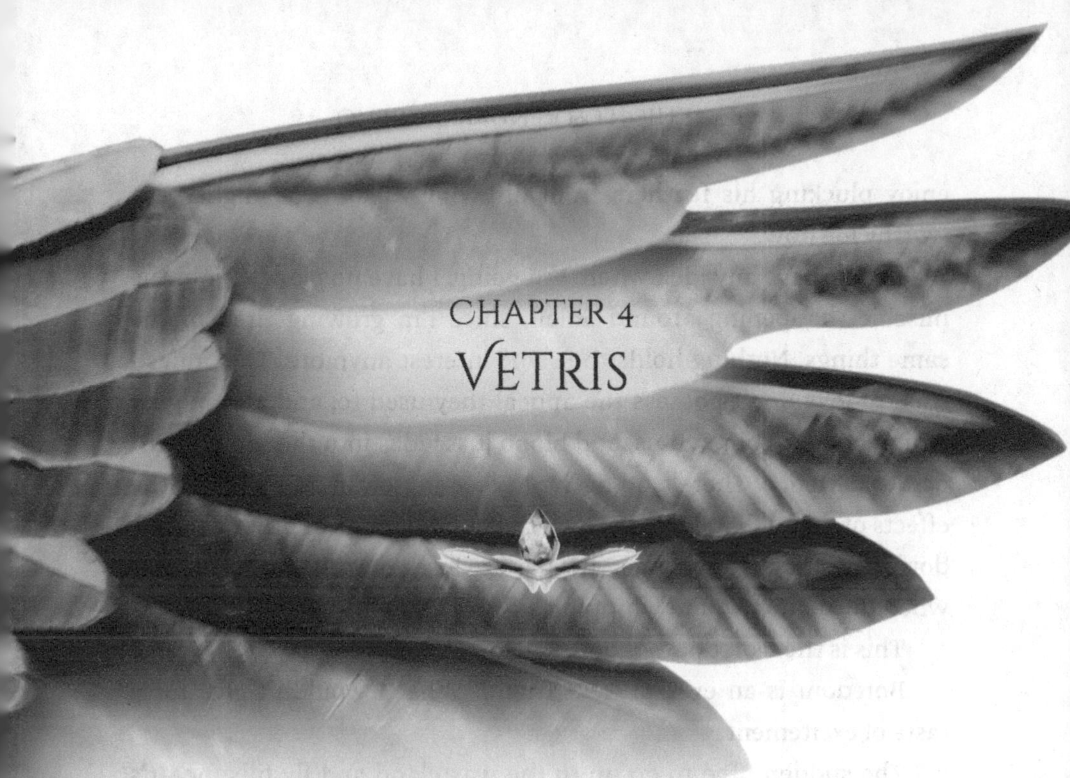

CHAPTER 4
VETRIS

Soleil never sleeps. Time has no bearing here. No matter the time of day or night, there is an orgy happening, some destruction taking place, or a party shaking the walls. The hellfire that climbs the walls vibrates with that energy, telling me that all is well within Soleil and that there is nothing to be worried about.

Not that I would care if there was.

Although I sit on the throne this year, it's not my responsibility to keep every minion in check. My duty is to be the leader, and to stand proud if we end up at war with someone else. I've hardly had to do much more than punish a rogue demon or two. Once, I had the pleasure of punishing an angel who sneaked into Soleil, thinking to cause trouble. I still remember Ajop's screams as I plucked his feathers. He returned to Celestia with damaged wings and the humiliation of being bested. It didn't affect him much though. I hear he's a dominion now. Only the best brownnosers become dominions, because they are the most easily manipulated.

Foolish angels.

Perhaps what we need is another good war after all. I'd certainly enjoy plucking his feathers from his wings again. He might be a worthy foe now.

I don't have any idea where I'm going. I have no plans to join the mischief happening around Soleil, since I'm growing tired of the same things. Nothing holds the same interest anymore. The orgies I used to love don't possess the appeal they used to, and all the glistening bodies, pain, whips, and blood just fades into the same mediocre experience. There's no desire to lose myself in ambrosia or the effects of demonbane either. Even the punishments of other demons don't do it for me any longer. It's hard to lose yourself in punishment when the demon you're whipping enjoys the destruction.

This is the worst part of living so long.

Boredom is an ever-present friend. What I wouldn't give for a taste of excitement.

The sudden urge to go up to the wasteland and fly fills me. It's been so long since I've flown, but I know the trouble it would cause. A crown prince soaring in the sky would start a war. They would take one look at my black feathered wings and the flaming crown atop my head and sound the trumpets.

Would a war be so bad?

We live beneath the soil like rodents, and we are kept here for what? Those islands in the sky might be a nice change. For once, those pompous feather brains can live in the fire. For once, they can feel the heat and live with it.

A group of death demons stumble from a tunnel to my right, each of them laughing and joking with each other.

"You saw the way that one bitch snapped her wings together in a huff," one comments. "I swear she was clenched so tight, the broom up her ass isn't going anywhere."

"Luckily for me, she snapped those wings when I told her I'd ride the broom right out of her," another replied with a laugh. He holds up a single, pale gray feather. "Now I have a trophy."

"The other one was—"

"Who are you talking about?" I ask, my eyes narrowed on the

single feather. No demon has feathers like that. Only princes and princesses have feathered wings down here, and none of us have light-colored feathers, which leaves only one option.

"Your holiness," they say as a unit, bending at the waist. The feather disappears behind his back, out of sight. "We didn't see you there. Forgive us—"

"Have you been to the wasteland?" I ask, raising my brow. I gesture for them to stand up so I can look them in the face, and they do so immediately.

They glance at each other, as if waiting to see who will answer. Finally, the first one to speak steps forward. "We were up there, your holiness, searching for a good time."

I tilt my head. "Judging by the feather the other one is hiding behind his back, you found one."

He visibly swallows. "Just a bit of fun, your holiness. We didn't harm the angel."

Sniffing, I tuck my wings in tight. "Pity. I could have used a good story to entertain me."

A slow smile crawls along his lips when he realizes he won't be punished. "Yes, your holiness. A pity indeed. Perhaps next time, we shall bring you a bouquet of feathers to entertain you."

I nod and move to leave. Demons. No matter the entertainment they have here in Soleil, they will always find new mischief. Of course, if that mischief gets them killed, it hardly matters to me. It only takes a moment of foolishness to end up dead. Death demons are only one step beneath the princes. If they die, there could be an imbalance, but they should be smart and strong enough to know better. Whatever they'd gotten up to, it clearly wasn't a problem if they lived to tell the tale.

"Show that feather off in the cauldron party, and it'll earn you free ambrosia for the night," I inform them before moving along.

"Thank you, your holiness," he wheezes. Something about the way his eyes shift to the others tells me there's more to the story, but I can't find it in me to care.

They are nothing more than petty demons searching for something to do. It's expected that they will grow tired of the confines of Soleil and seek others. At any moment, they can leave Soleil and go through the portal, which many choose to do.

Here, we live beneath the surface, but on the other side of the portal, demons have free rein—within reason, though there are other forces who keep our kind in check there. At least there, though, they are free and they can fly.

Here, we're nothing more than bothersome ants beneath the ground.

The urge to fly and find an angel to take my frustration out on is strong.

I'm the crown prince, however, so instead I disappear into my chambers.

I sleep through the most raucous party in years, according to Manon when I wake up, but even that doesn't bother me.

The crackling of the flames gets on my nerves and slowly drives me insane.

CHAPTER 5
ROUX

As I am led away, I can't help but plead my innocence, even if I know I should remain quiet to maintain my dignity like we are taught.

I don't. I yell as they drag me down the dimly lit path toward the dungeons. It's a place not many visit. Angels misbehave, that's true, but usually one night in there is enough to put them back on track. I know it won't be one night for me, not after... not after they are framing me for the theft of something.

No, I will be in the dungeons until they decide to kill me.

I know if I go through those doors, I'm dead, so I start to fight.

It's the only reason none of us see her until it's too late. Brandishing a huge wooden pole, she slams it into both angels holding me.

Rosa quickly knocks them both out, leaving me wide-eyed and gaping as she smiles at me shyly. Hurrying over, she unfastens my wings and hands, but I still don't move. My eyes go from her to the unconscious angels. "They will kill you for that," I whisper. "Quickly, rechain me. They didn't see you. I will take the blame—"

"No, go, Roux. Escape. I will not let them blame you. It is too late for me. My fate was always to be their whipping girl, but you can be so much more." Her eyes dart around, scanning for threats as she grabs my arm and hauls me to the edge of the island. I shouldn't be surprised that she's strong. After all, she has to be to work with the blacksmith. "Go now!"

"Where to?" I ask, lost and confused.

"The only place you can—Earth. Go through the portal. There's one in the wasteland. You've seen it, yes?" she asks, and I nod numbly. "Good. Go through it and find somewhere safe, where they can't reach you. If you stay, they'll kill you, Roux." She starts to back away as light spreads near the unconscious angels. The others are searching for the perpetrator and me. Cupping her mouth, she starts to yell, "Over here, you angel assholes. Let's see if you can catch me!" With one last look at me, she smiles sadly. "I have repaid your kindness, Roux. Do not let that be in vain. Go!" With that, she starts to run in the opposite direction, drawing the searching guards toward her.

I hesitate and debate chasing after her, but she made her choice.

So I make mine.

I turn and throw myself from the island and into the dark sky below.

Rosa is right. I know where the portal is, every angel and demon does, and I head there now, not taking the time to enjoy the flight or look around for what might be my last time here. No, I fly there and land just before it. With a final panicked look up at Celestia, I throw myself through.

I HAVE BEEN through a portal before, but it's not something you ever truly get used to. It spits me out on Earth, in the Amazon rainforest to be exact. I take a quick look around, noting the lush green trees overhead and the invisible net barrier sparkling with magic to stop angels and demons from flying off before being spoken to. Huts crowd amongst the trees, filled with bars and staff housing. The humidity hits me instantly, making me sweat as I gather my wings together. I'll be seen as a threat if I don't.

All I have is myself, and I must look as lost as I feel. A whistling portal guard notices me and heads over, only to stop and tilt her head as she takes me in.

I do the same to her, worried she will try to send me back through. Her hair is unusual, an ombre blue color that catches the moonlight, and her skin is light brown. Her dark brown eyes scan me from head to toe, and then she sighs. "Need sanctuary?" she drawls.

I nod silently.

"Don't tell me," she starts before I can speak the truth. "It's better if I don't know so I won't have answers when they come after you. Look, I know somewhere you can go."

"Why would you help me?" I finally ask.

For a moment, her eyes darken before she shakes it off and smiles sadly. "Let's call it women sticking together, but you don't look like trouble, more like someone stuck in the middle. I won't tell them where you went." She pulls a parchment from her bag and quickly writes something down before handing it over. "Go there. Tell them I sent you. You'll be safe for a little while, at least until you figure out your next move."

"Thank you..." I trail off.

"Adora." She grins. "Name's Adora Kresley. Yours?"

"Roux," I reply. "Thank you." I fold the paper carefully and, with one last look at the portal, slide past her.

"Better hurry now. You don't want to be here when they come after you."

Heeding her warning, I begin to run through the trees, having to keep my wings tucked in tight to avoid being hurt. When I pass the barrier of the five-mile wide net, I burst up through the trees and into the night sky, heading to the place on the piece of paper.

I hope I'll find safety from my own kind, because I'll be seen as a traitor now. I have no one, but I have a location—No Man's Land Circus.

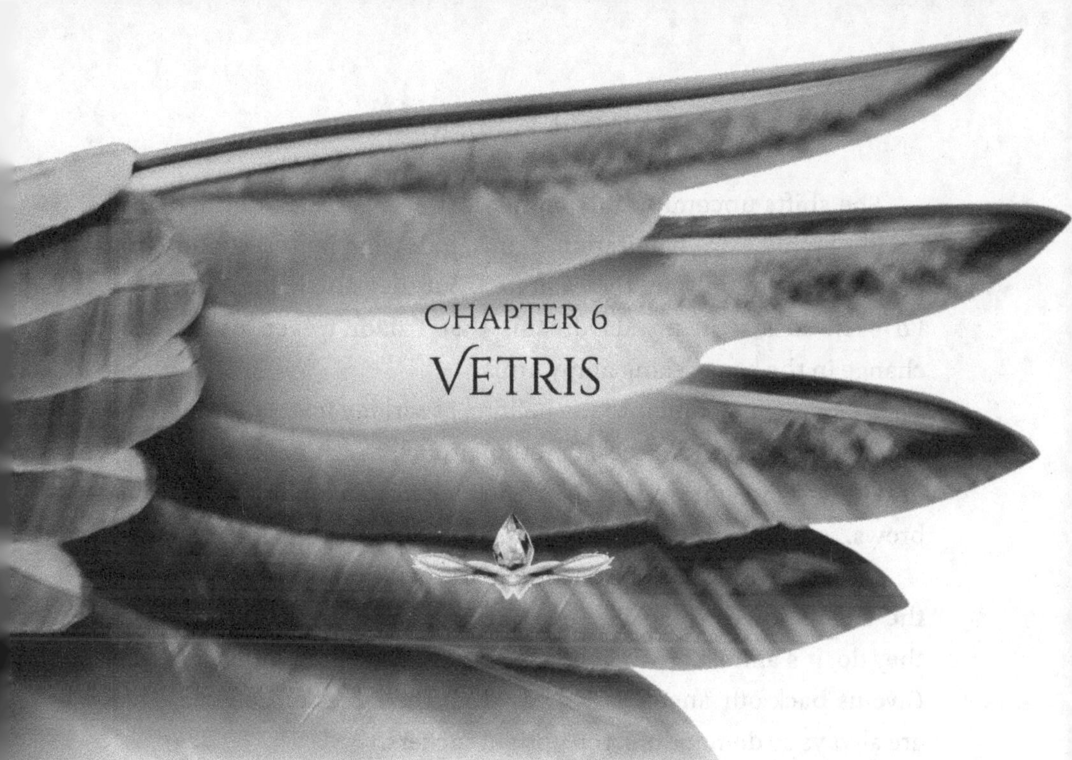

CHAPTER 6
VETRIS

Another boring ass day. Even the throne feels uncomfortable today. The bones of the arms dig into my thighs where I drape my legs over them, annoying me in a way that makes me grind my teeth. Why does it feel like everything from my skin to my wingtips is aching for... something? Have I really gotten so old that this is all I can manage to handle?

I'm barely a minute away from storming out of the throne room, but I'm required to be available as the crown prince for at least a few hours, and going on a rampage through Soleil would prevent me from fulfilling that duty. Any demon who dares to get in my path will suffer the consequences. I'll rip their spines from their bodies and wave them around like a weapon. I'll flay their skin from their bones and make a new throw blanket. I'll burn them with the hellfire that—

"Your Majesty?"

The voice breaks me out of my musings and draws me back to the present. I blink my eyes to clear the vision, and Manon comes into focus.

I scowl. "What the fuck do you want?"

She shifts uncomfortably on her feet and gestures to the flames licking up my skin in agitation. I turn, following her gaze, and blink in surprise. Not only are they agitated, but they also bring a message. I'd been so lost in my daydreams that I hadn't even noticed the change in the heat licking at my arms.

Reaching my hand into the hellfire, I twirl my fingers through the flames and wait until I feel something touch my fingers. Once I do, I draw my hand out and stare at the singed parchment with raised brows.

"A message from Celestia," I remark, grinning. It isn't often that the angels lower themselves to correspond with Soleil, but when they do, it's almost always entertaining. Keep your demons in check. Give us back our angel. Stay away from the edges of Celestia. They are always so demanding, the uptight fuckers.

"What is it?" Manon asks curiously, her eyes on the parchment in my hands.

I bare my teeth at the succubus. "Keep your nose where it belongs, Manon."

She harrumphs, and I can tell she wants to argue, but instead, she settles back into her lounge. I don't know how she can stand to lie around like that so much. It's driving me insane, while these demons are content with doing nothing.

Carefully, I unroll the parchment and stare at the words written in elegant, pompous script.

Prince Vetris,

The angels require your unique skills to hunt down an angelic traitor of the utmost importance. She must be brought back to Celestia promptly before she sows dishonor in other weak angels. I expect you to find this angel, Roux, and bring her to Celestia for her punishment, alive. She has taken something of utmost value. Your cooperation will be rewarded.

Signed,

Rael

• • •

A LETTER from one of the Seraphim. My brows rise impossibly high at the tone of the letter and the demand within. My immediate instinct is to decline. Fuck the angels and their holier than thou bullshit. I want nothing to do with them.

But hunting an angel without repercussions and with full permission? I can even rough her up a bit and teach her a lesson, as long as she arrives alive, which is the only stipulation. That would cure my boredom far faster than anything else. It's been so long since I've tracked. It's been even longer since I've used my special skills on an angel.

Laughter bubbles out of my throat. "Do you know what this means, Manon?"

She sniffs. "How could I when you wouldn't tell me what's in the letter?"

"I've been ordered to hunt an angel. The seraphim is demanding I find her and bring her back to Celestia." I shake my head, wearing a cruel smile.

"Demanded? Does he think he rules Soleil?" Manon shakes her head. "Foolish seraphim."

"Perhaps," I muse. "But I'm going to do it anyway. If only for the opportunity to put one of their own in their place." My lips curl up savagely. "Maybe I'll play with her before I return her to Celestia. I might enjoy myself then."

Manon's answering smile feeds my own. "Will you let me play, too, Your Majesty? I would very much like to play."

I stand and toss the parchment back into the hellfire, my answer scrawled in aggressive script along the bottom. "We'll see, succubus." I spread my wings wide. "We'll see."

I step from the throne room, excitement thrumming in my veins, but I can already tell this chase will be unique. They never would have contacted me if this Roux was still in our world. She's gone through the portal, and I'm going to hunt her down. Angels hate lowering themselves to visit Earth, something about the divine balance or being closer to their god—who the fuck cares.

Even if I detest going through portals as much as they do, I will gladly do it.

"I'll return," I tell Manon. "And when I do, make sure the throne room is prepared for some fun."

Manon grins as I move through Soleil, my wings itching to fly.

For the first time in too long, there's an extra hop in my step and a smile remains on my face.

It's time to hunt an angel.

CHAPTER 7
ROUX

The circus is easier to find than I would have thought. I have to fly for a few days, barely taking any breaks, too worried they are following me. It leaves me irritable and in desperate need of rest and food when I land before the big top. The sun is high in the sky, so the ground is mostly covered with dead, leftover confetti, along with banners and flyers. There are closed stalls and games everywhere, and the big top stands high and proud in the middle.

It's quiet.

The crumbling apartment building around it is also quiet, and I worry I was sent to the wrong place. For a moment, my eyes linger on the Ferris wheel, standing tall and proud. It's all so clean and well maintained. There has to be people here.

Well, clean might be a stretch.

It's half destroyed, like most buildings in this world now. Angels try to stay out of the houses' business as much as possible, but I know enough to know this has to be out of their control.

Neutral, or so I hope.

I've watched this world rise and fall, watched so much death and destruction, yet there is an odd beauty to Earth, to its resistance, and its need to survive. As the darkness, and those in the dark, took over and created order, I found myself slipping through the portal more and more to watch it be rebuilt. Now, it's divided amongst the different species into those very houses I am trying to avoid.

It's not like I can waltz into House of Air and Amethyst, which the angels have an affiliation with, or even House of Gold and Garnet, where the demons they know would kill me on sight.

No, I'm on my own and standing in the middle of a circus.

"Hello?" I call hesitantly as I tuck in my wings. "I mean no harm."

"That's good, because you would be dead before you could succeed," a dark voice says, and then stepping from the big top is what I can only describe as a ringmaster, who's in a flashy getup to match. Rosa and I once snuck through and saw some traveling shows. The other ringmasters were nowhere as flashy as this, but I can still recognize that this is the man in charge, and if my powers are correct, he's a shifter of some kind.

They tend to be hot-headed but trustworthy, so I tilt my chin back and smile. "Hi, what's your name?"

"I'm the Ringmaster, and you are lost."

"No, I was seeking this place. I met someone who suggested I could find shelter here. I need sanctuary."

"We don't take in strays." The Ringmaster states.

Irritation winds through me, as does exhaustion and fear. I haven't stopped running since my sentence was passed, and I have no doubt they are hunting me. I need to regroup, rest, and figure out a plan, and this man is standing in my way. Maybe that's why my retort comes out sharper and less refined than normal, but an angel always knows her wants and needs. This shifter is no exception.

"Then let me work for it. I only need to lie low for a few days until I can come up with a plan." His eyes run over me in a clinical manner as I speak. "I bet you've never had any angels before, have you?" I see his eye twitch, and I know I'm right. "Room and board for a few days, and I'll be an act for one night."

"Two nights for every three days you stay," he barters.

"Deal." I offer him my hand.

Grumbling, he takes it and shakes it quickly before letting me go. He holds his arm out dramatically as he bows and says, "Welcome to No Man's Land Circus, runaway."

~

THE APARTMENT I'm shown to is tiny. It only holds a bed, a dresser, and a small kitchenette.

It's perfect.

I flop onto the bed, groaning as I stretch out my wings and let my muscles relax. Flying can be tiring without breaks, and right now, my body is screaming at me for pushing it too hard. I lie here for a moment before I drag myself up.

I shower and dress in some clothes that are left by my door—tight black jeans, a human creation that I quite like, and then a loose top with strings that go around my neck, left open at the back for my wings. The front is a flowing, white silk material only held together between my breast with a button, leaving most of my midriff and chest on display. It doesn't bother me, and I can admit it matches my wings as I twirl. I devour the food they leave, and then I sprawl out once more.

I need to figure out my next move, but before I can, my awareness fades, and I slip into a much needed sleep.

"Well, looky here, a little angel all spread out just for me." The drawling voice has me jerking up and reaching for my sword that isn't there anymore. My heart slams to a stop, and my runes light up with my power as my eyes focus on the demon before me.

I have no idea how he found me or how he got in here past the wards unless he's unaffected by the magic, but there is no doubt in my mind about what he is.

His huge black wings are tucked away, the feathers ending in a red tip that tells me he's more powerful than I could hope for. Fire crawls along his well-built, muscular arms, which are partially hidden under a leather duster jacket. He's tall, easily six-eight, with muscles upon muscles concealed beneath tight black clothing and boots. I spot scars littering his skin, but my eyes are locked on his face.

He's beautiful, in a fallen angel, soul stealing kind of way.

His black eyes are surrounded by thick lashes. He has a strong jaw and sharp cheekbones, and horns protrude from the front of his forehead, surrounded by luscious black hair with a streak of orange.

No lower demon would lean there so casually, and not even a higher one would be this cocky when it comes to an angel.

No, he is something else, and a burst of fear flows through me at the realization of who this might be.

"What do you want?" I demand haughtily, trying my best not to show my worry.

"Angels, always thinking they are in charge," he scoffs. "You know that holier than thou attitude isn't going to save you, right?"

"Save me? You're here to kill me?" I demand with a strange detachment in my voice as I get to my feet, refusing to be cowed.

"Oh no, little angel. I'm here to drag you back to hell, kicking and screaming." He smirks, his tongue darting out to trace his lips as he eyes my outfit.

"You want me to beg you not to?" I spit. "Beg for my life? I won't."

"I do like begging, but usually when I'm balls deep in a woman." He laughs. "But your begging isn't necessary. It won't change anything."

"Why are you helping the angels?" I demand, because if he's here for me, then he has to be. This isn't a coincidence. "Are demons truly so dumb that they follow their orders and blindly listen to them?" I taunt.

He wags his finger at me, not the least bit ruffled. "That's not very nice. I thought angels were supposed to be all love and sunshine and shit. I'm not doing this for the angels, unicorn. Did you really think you were such a good guy?" The chuckle he releases makes me cross my arms in anger, which puts my hand near the plate I was eating from earlier. "How naïve of you. Now, easy way or hard way?" He runs his eyes over me once more. "I know which I would prefer."

"You want me?" I grab the plate as I lean forward, distracting him, and just like I thought, his eyes drop to my boobs. "You'll have to fucking catch me," I snarl as I throw the plate and leap into the air.

It shatters across his face, sending him spinning around. I yank open the door, and I'm halfway through it when an arm bands around my waist and yanks me back in. My breath leaves my body as he slams me against it and presses me to the wood. The strength and the warmth in his body as he effortlessly holds me makes me spit and hiss like a wild animal.

I'm trapped.

"Really, unicorn? That all you got?" I freeze when warm breath blows over my ear and lips run down my throat in a sensual tease I'm not prepared for. "I'm disappointed."

Closing my eyes for a moment, I let my power surge through me, and when I open them, I know they glow from within. "Yes? Well, you're about to be a whole lot happier."

I slam my wings open at the same time I fling my power at him, letting it fill the room around us violently.

Angel one, demon zero.

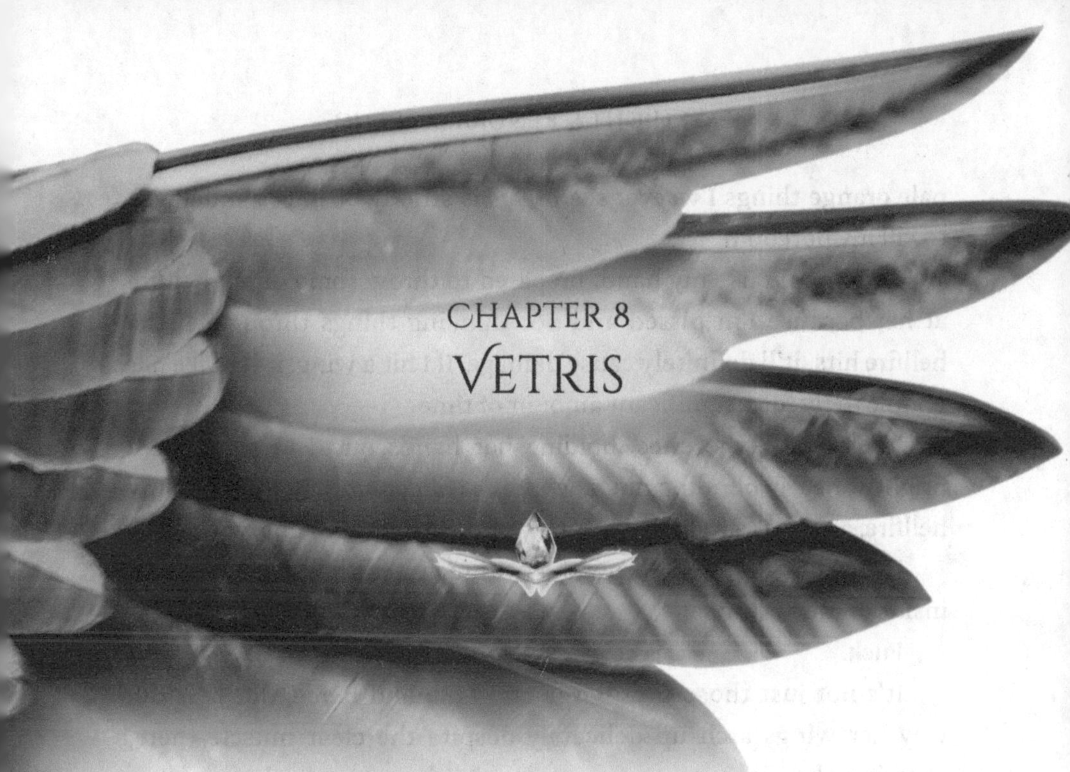

CHAPTER 8
VETRIS

How long has it been since I've felt the full power of an archangel? Fuck, I don't even remember when it last happened. Perhaps back when the war took place between Soleil and Celestia, I encountered the warrior angels who fight as viciously as they worship, but I've grown complacent. In my arrogance, and with the pretty features of the angel before me, I'd forgotten just how powerful an archangel can be.

Until her magic slams into me, that is.

It's more powerful because she's desperate and clearly hoping to get away. The runes along her skin light up in pretty symbols, the pure white light filling the room seconds before her wings snap open and all that power in her small body hits me.

I'm sent flying backwards, and my back slams against the rickety dresser against the wall. I grunt at the bite of pain, and then my own wings snap open in anger, the hellfire on my arms flaring brightly in response to being hit with her holy magic. Her eyes widen at the sight, at the demonic image I probably create, but I don't care. I don't care how pretty her eyes are or that her wings are the softest fucking pale orange things I've ever seen. This is strictly business and a way to kill my boredom.

Snarling, I raise my hand, prepared to throw some of my hellfire at her because I'm pissed and not thinking things through. If the hellfire hits, it'll definitely cause damage. If I hit a wing, it'll make her unable to fly for a significant amount of time.

"No! Wait!" she cries, holding her hands out. Her runes flare brightly, nearly blinding me. The room is filled with her light and my hellfire, a threat, a reflection of the war once fought in our world.

Just as I'm about to throw the hellfire at her, though, something inside of me hesitates.

Fuck.

It's not just those eyes, large and blue and fierce, nor is it the way her wings arch up delicately despite the clear muscle there, showing the signs of a warrior angel. It's not even the way her hips flare out from her waist, or the way her shirt reveals her breasts.

It's something deeper than that.

The only thing I can think of is hatred. We both hate each other so much, angel against demon, bright against dark, that my gut is telling me not to destroy her because it would be unfair. After all, she's only an archangel, and I'm the crown prince. I've been tasked with bringing her in. It would be pitiful to kill her when she's provided such entertainment already.

The hellfire settles down as I straighten and tug on my shirt, pulling out the wrinkles. "It matters not," I state. "You're coming with me, unicorn."

She wrinkles her nose up at me. "Why do you keep calling me that?" She seems to think better of her question and waves her hand through the air. "Never mind. Look, I get it. Someone sent you after me because I'm some sort of... some sort of..."

"Traitor," I supply helpfully, amused at her floundering.

"Yes, well, I'm not," she growls. "I'm being framed. I didn't steal anything, only witnessed it. Look, if you just help me—"

I laugh. "Help you? An angel? You've lost your pretty little mind, unicorn."

She grits her teeth at the nickname but doesn't rise to the bait. "There's some sort of orb. I saw angels and demons talking in the wasteland. They were making a deal—"

"Demons don't make deals with angels."

"And yet here you are," she points out, and it makes me frown. "I'm not asking for you to believe me. I'm sure this is amusing for you, or it's a way to get your jollies off, but help me find this orb and clear my name, and I'll make it worth your while."

I raise my brows. "Oh? And pray tell, unicorn. What is it you have that you think I want?" My eyes trace down her body, taking in everything from her thin neck to her supple hips before going back up. "I'm a prince, so you'll have to make it good."

Her expression doesn't change at my admittance of station. She probably already assumed I was so high, but I lose some satisfaction when her eyes don't widen and her nose doesn't flare. I was so hoping for some surprise.

Pity.

At my innuendo, the suggestion that she has her body to barter, she puts her hands on her hips, and her wings flare in agitation. "What do you think you want?"

The smile that curls my lips makes her shift on her feet. Oh, so the little angel isn't unaffected. Interesting. Interesting, indeed. My instinct is to tell her to get on her knees and open her mouth, so I can fuck her mouth until I feel more compliant and willing, but somehow, I don't think she'll be so submissive. Pity. Imagining her on her knees before me stirs something deep in my core, a need, a want, and I'm surprised by it. She's an angel, a sworn enemy, and I've been tasked with hunting her down as a traitor. I shouldn't want to pin her against the wall and fuck her until she worships me instead of her precious seraphim.

I tell myself it's the draw of the angels, all the sparkle and beauty, but it's also the fire in her eyes. How adorable that one of the warrior angels is rebelling, and that she spouts tales of being framed and angels working with demons. After all these years, one of them finally got wise and saw through their blessed leaders. And this orb? This thing she's searching for? If the seraphim want it so badly they are willing to blame this angel who proclaims her innocence, then it must be powerful.

A tool like that in the hands of Soleil could be just what we need.

"I don't suppose you'll give me that sweet, holy pussy as payment?" I suggest anyways, if only to see her eyes flare in disgust.

Instead, I'm surprised when her mask stays firmly in place. Not even her eyes widen. But the scent? Oh, how interesting. What an intriguing concept, an angel aroused by a demon.

Hatred is a toxic drug for fucking. Apparently, I'm not the only one considering how brutal and perfect sex between enemies can be.

"Get fucked," she says, and it's my turn to be surprised.

My eyes widen, and a startled laugh slips out. "Do you talk to your precious seraphim that way?" I tease. A growl is my answer, and it only makes my amusement grow. This could be interesting. "Fine. I'll help you find the orb."

"You will?" she asks, her eyes narrowing in suspicion.

"If," I continue, holding up my hand, "you keep being the adorable little rebel you are."

She tips up her chin. "And?"

"And I get first dibs on the orb."

"Out of the question," she growls. "I'm trying to prove I'm innocent. Giving it to a demon would just condemn me again."

I grin. "Then the deal is off."

She huffs, her shoulders tense. "You can have it for a day."

"A week," I counter, "and you have to spend the entire week with me in Soleil, including the time it takes for us to track down this orb in the first place."

She crosses her arms. "What do you hope to accomplish by caging me, demon?"

I stroll forward, watching her tense the closer I get until I'm right in front of her, only a small breath of air between us. My wings are larger than hers, more imposing, but she doesn't tuck her wings in and cower when I take up the space of this tiny apartment. If anything, she widens her own stance and spreads her wings to show me she's not some meek lower angel.

She's a warrior for a reason.

"Tell me, unicorn," I murmur as I lean down, my breath dancing across her cheek and drawing a bit of color to her skin. "How does it feel to know your leaders are not as perfect as you assumed? How does it feel to fall?"

She tilts her head and meets my eyes, unflinching and unafraid despite the hellfire dancing along my arms. "I assume it feels as painful as taking orders from your mortal enemy," she retorts, her voice steady. "How does it feel to be on your knees for the seraphim despite your nobility?"

I grin and run my tongue along my teeth. "There's only one reason I'd ever be on my knees, little angel," I murmur, "and that's because I would be sliding my tongue between your folds, flicking your clit until you screamed for Soleil's crown prince and the runes on your skin flared with your ecstasy." Her cheeks turn crimson, but she doesn't pull away. "And when you finished screaming for me, I'd show you just how holy it can be to fall."

She scoffs. "Angels don't fall."

Chuckling darkly, I back away, giving her space, but not before I gesture to the door for her to lead the way on this new hunt, this new cure for my boredom. For the first time in decades, my body sings with excitement.

"Oh, but you will, unicorn," I purr, meeting the fire in her eyes and relishing the tint to her skin. "I can promise you that."

CHAPTER 9
ROUX

I hate him.

It's more than the fact that he's a demon prince, which is terrifying, because I know how powerful they can be. No, it's the fact that he called me on my bullshit and that my body is thrumming with hatred and desire—desire I have no right feeling for the cocky, smirking prince before me. For a moment, I almost swayed into him. I'd rather die before I acted upon this strange desire between us. It cannot happen.

I will clear my name and be welcomed back with open arms... um, wings, and fucking a crown prince of our enemies is a good way to go. I would be damned forever, and the crown prince would throw me away like a broken plaything.

I see it in his glowing eyes. He relishes pain and destruction, and I will not let him destroy me.

He has another thing coming if he thinks I'm some meek little angel he can ruin. He might think he has the upper hand because I need his help, but I'm the one who has it. Crown princes are notoriously good at tracking, hence why he found me. It will make finding this orb easier, and I'll survive the time at his side and walk back into

Celestia with the orb. I'll prove I'm worthy of my title and can do more than they think.

"Where do we start?" I tilt my chin back, refusing to cower before his power and station. I can almost see the crown of fire sitting atop his messy hair.

"I can think of some things." He runs his tongue along his lips, and the sneer he gives me makes my lips curl, even as my clit throbs with desire. Chuckling like he senses it, he gestures at the door once more. "I meant starting with leaving this..." He looks around in derision. "Is this a cupboard?"

"It's an apartment," I spit. "Sorry it's not good enough for you, your holy damnation." I bow mockingly, my attitude rising to meet his. It's almost second nature.

He laughs. "That's better." He pats my head as he passes. "Come on, unicorn. Let's find this orb, and then we can work on your submissiveness."

"I will never submit to you," I sneer as I rip open the door and storm out, feeling him trailing after me. So much for staying on the down low at the circus and figuring out my next move, but even as I think that, I realize I wouldn't have known where to start.

As much as I hate it, I need his help.

"We'll see about that, pretty angel," he purrs right in my ear. Turning at the tone of his voice, I slam him into the wall, watching his eyes flare with interest and anger. "Careful, unicorn, don't want to burn those pretty wings," he taunts, completely unaffected by my show of force.

Something about him just ruffles my feathers. Leaning in, I snarl, "Cut the shit, demon. Let's just find the orb, and if you so much as touch me, I'll kill you."

"You could try, and wouldn't that be magnificent?" he purrs.

"Fucking demons," I mutter as I release him and stomp downstairs, past the communal rooms, and out into the carnival that seems to be waking up. People are moving around everywhere, no doubt preparing for tonight's show—a show I should be in. I almost wince at the fact that I'm going back on my deal. Angels always keep their promises, but I don't think the crown prince will wait as I perform for the crowd. Instead, I launch into the air before they can stop me, feeling him trail behind with a husky laugh.

"It's ironic that an archangel lowered herself to hide within a den of debauchery and tricks," he calls as he swoops around me, flying in circles.

"They offered me sanctuary," I retort.

"And what did you offer them, hmm?" He stops before me, flames crawling along his spread wings as a smile curves his lips.

For a moment, I just stare despite the fact we are enemies. I should hate him, but he is beautiful.

Achingly so.

"You'll never know," I tease as I swoop under him.

"Oh, unicorn, this is going to be fun!" he calls after me.

~

I'M GOING to kill him.

Lounging on a park bench, he licks his ice cream in the most indecent way as he watches me pace. "We need to be tracking, not eating!"

"There is always time for *eating*." He emphasizes the word, making me flare my wings before I force myself to calm down.

Do not kill him. Do not start a war.

"I'd love to see you try. You know, you're very easy to wind up. You angels are so high-strung. You just need a few good orgasms, unicorn."

Yes, I'm going to kill him.

I whirl, intending to give him a piece of my mind, only to suddenly find him before me. He thrusts the ice cream toward my lips. "It's cotton candy with nectar," he says in a chipper voice. I have no choice but to taste it when it touches my lips, and he grins, but then his smile drops and his eyes darken as he watches me lick the remnants from my lips. “Fucking hell,” he mutters.

“Yes, exactly. I’m in hell. Please, can we find the orb?”

We stopped at the nearest city, but we are trying to remain out of the houses’ notice, or anyone’s to be honest. An angel and a demon working together? Word would soon get back through the portal, which is not what I need, and neither does he. The seraphim would not be happy to learn what we’re doing here.

He tilts his head as he watches me. “I need something to go on to track it. That’s how I work.”

“I have nothing. I don’t even know what it is!”

“Then we need to find someone who does,” he replies like it’s simple. “I know someone, a librarian. We will ask him. Happy now, angel face?”

“Not since the moment your fiery ass stepped foot near me,” I mutter.

“For an angel, you’re not very nice.” He grins. “I like it. Shakes up the status quo. Okay then, unicorn, follow me.” He shoots into the air with a flair only a crown prince of Soleil can have.

“Show-off,” I mutter as I launch after him.

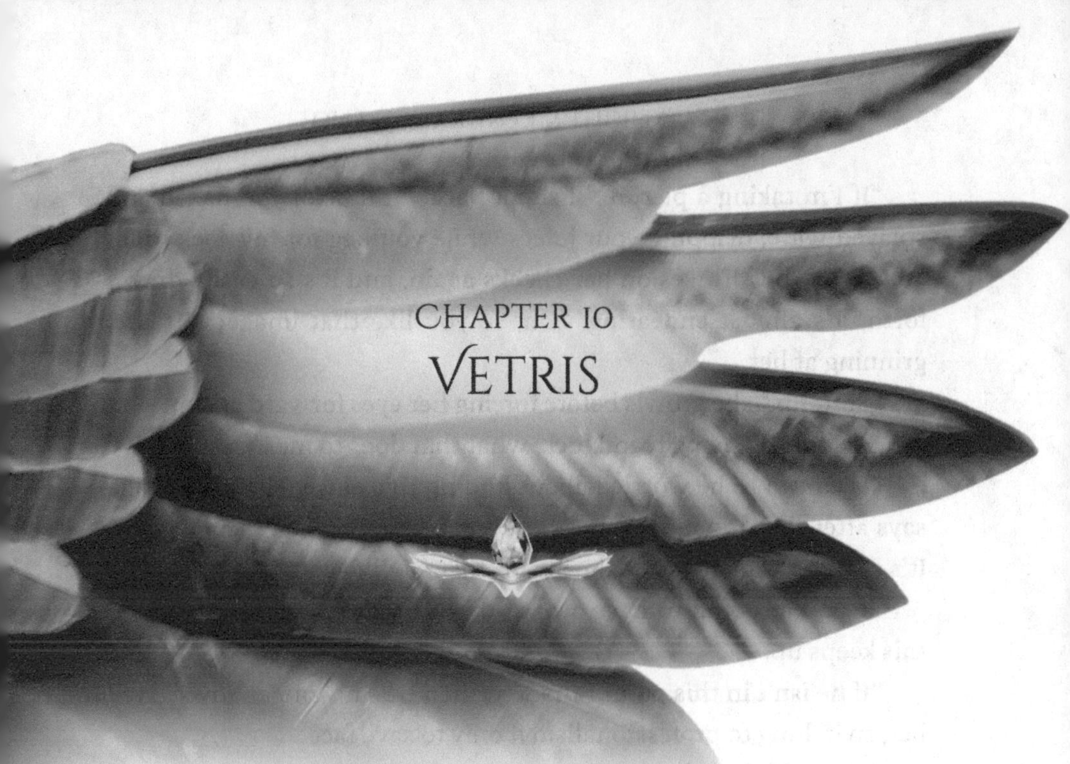

CHAPTER 10
VETRIS

Three days, three long insufferable days.

That's how long I've had the "pleasurable" company of the rebellious angel currently walking by my side. Every chance she gets, she needles me, but for every barb her tongue whips out, I return the favor tenfold, ruffling her feathers every chance I get.

I have to say, despite the annoyance, I'm far from the boredom I felt before this hunt. For once, I'm not thinking about the end of my reign. I'm far more entranced by the angel currently scowling at me for staring at her for longer than is proper.

"Why don't you take a picture?" she grumbles. "Maybe it'll last longer."

I snort at the look in her eyes, at the annoyance and heat there. We've danced around it, but fuck if I haven't imagined taking her every which way. The desire to see those lush lips wrapped around my cock has only grown the longer I'm in her presence. I'm sure it has more to do with putting an enemy on her knees than it has anything to do with Roux herself.

I've had to tell myself that often lately.

"If I'm taking a picture," I shoot back, "it'll be of you naked and splayed wide, dripping your juices while you beg for my cock to fill you." That blush rises on her cheeks again, and it's so easily drawn forth, it's almost endearing. "Oh, so you like that image?" I tease, grinning at her.

"Shut up," she growls before forcing her eyes forward again.

She doesn't deny it, and fuck, what that does to me...

"We need to be worried about finding this elusive librarian," she says after that moment hangs between us, not even glancing at me. It's as if she wants to hide the blush still crawling across her cheeks.

Fuck, I'm going to have a hard-on in the middle of the street if this keeps up.

"If he isn't in this part of the city, then he's no longer alive," I tell her, switching to professionalism if only to save face.

"You said that about the last three locations," she points out, her gaze finally swinging to me, and I get the glorious sight of her brilliant blue eyes combined with the flush of her cheeks. "Maybe you don't know what you're doing."

"Or maybe it's not an exact science," I retort, annoyed. "Keep in mind that I'm doing you a favor and can choose to change my mind at any time."

"We made a deal," she argues, her face hardening, as if she's prepared to fight me despite the power imbalance. Surely an archangel would know she stands no chance against a crown prince of Soleil.

I shoot her a lecherous grin. "I'm the demon here for a reason, unicorn."

She hesitates for a moment, as if unsure what to make of that. "Good to know my assumptions of your kind are correct."

"Indeed," I growl, despite knowing that I wouldn't go back on my deal. A demon's word is all he has, and I pride myself on fulfilling my promises. Just as I intend to keep our deal, I also intend to have Roux on her knees, begging for a taste.

A crown prince always keeps his word.

Her runes dance to life on her skin, not because she feels threatened, but because she's on alert as we grow closer to our destination. The strange club is in the middle of the seedy side of the city, where the roads aren't cleaned and trash flies by in the wind. The world is a little sadder here, a little unkempt, and the humans who exist here are down on their luck. The librarian prefers these types of areas. It's easier to hide when no one bothers to come looking. Most of the houses wouldn't dare to come look here. They wouldn't lower themselves like this.

As we enter the darker side of the city, I expect Roux to cringe away from the homeless humans along the buildings, their faces dirty and unwashed, their eyes haunted with their trauma. I expect her to flinch away when one of them reaches for her wing, amazed by the sparkly beauty of her.

"An angel," an elderly man rasps, his mouth missing all but a few teeth. "I always thought it would be an angel who would come for me." His fingers brush the tip of Roux's wing, and I wait for her to explode, to scream, to grimace. Instead, I'm surprised yet again.

Roux stops immediately and looks down at the man before squatting in front of him, her eyes bright with empathy. "I'm afraid I have not come for you this time, sir, but there will be better days. I can promise you that." I watch as she reaches up to the wing he touches and traces her fingers along the feather there. She stiffens for a split second before she jerks the feather free, a pain I know all too well. She lifts the feather between them and smiles. "For you," she offers. "To lead the way out of your misery."

The man's eyes widen, and despite his situation and what this could mean, he starts to shake his head. "I cannot take—"

"You can," Roux says firmly. "It's a gift from an angel to a man. I offer it freely."

The man grimaces. "What do you want for it?"

"Only a promise that you'll use it to help yourself," she replies, her smile still gentle. "I see your strength and your longing. You are not forgotten, Benjamin. You are not lost."

"How did you..." The man trails off, realizing he's talking to a human and that Roux's powers might stretch to reading his mind. He swallows, and his hand twitches. "I have a daughter who wears angel wings and says she's going to fly one day. I'm not allowed to see her when I look like this, but with this gift, you're giving me the chance to spend time with her again. She's been waiting, so full of hope..."

Roux reaches forward and touches his shoulder gently. "She'll fly one day, Benjamin. Just like she believes in you, I believe in you." She stands. "I must leave you. I wish you the best luck in this world."

His hands cradle the feather to his chest, hiding it from other eyes, knowing what a precious item he holds. "Thank you, love. Thank you."

Roux gestures for us to continue. Not once does she wipe her hand in disgust despite the man smelling like week old yogurt. Not once does she flinch away from the others who reach for her in their delusions.

"Why did you do that?" I ask, staring at her as if I've never met her before. I've seen seraphim walk among humans. I've seen angels who come to Earth and walk among them. There is always disgust on their faces, contempt for a race that can't help their plight.

"Do what?" she answers, frowning at me.

"Surely you know what a feather like yours is worth here?"

She nods. "I do."

"And you just ripped it out and gave it to a human? Let him profit from your beauty?"

"Someone should profit from it, no?" She glances over at me. "Which building are we going to?"

She changes the subject as if she didn't just change some human's life. That feather will fetch a large price. If he's smart, he'll be able to get away from this part of town, clean himself up, see his daughter again, and get a job. She gave him the gift of a new beginning.

And she asked for nothing in return.

"It's an act, isn't it?" I growl, furrowing my brows at her. "It has to be."

"What are you talking about?" she asks, clearly surprised by my outburst.

"Angels don't just give away their feathers, and certainly not to humans. They don't act like that. They are cruel and callous. They are petty and pompous. This is all an act."

Roux stares at me. Those blue eyes take in everything from the expression on my face to the tension in my wings. I feel exposed in ways I've never felt, and it grinds my nerves, but I don't say anything or she'll win. This act is getting to me far more than the little barbs and disdain when she looks at me. I've watched her precious seraphim walk over bodies of humans like dirt, and here she is, choosing ones to help and taking the hands of any who reach for her.

She is what an angel should be.

"That man doesn't belong here," she finally says, her runes dancing with her power. It strokes along mine, clashes with it, and the hellfire along my arms dances with our combined agitation.

"And the others do?" I growl in frustration.

She dips her chin. "Some of them, yes, but not him. If I can help one unfortunate soul, then I've done my duty."

"Your duty is to Celestia," I point out.

"My duty is to goodness," she counters. "My duty is to help where I am able. Now which building are we going to before I decide to kick your ass in the middle of the street? I'm sure the feathers of a crown prince will fetch a nice price too. Let's see what happens when I rip them out."

The threat is snarled, her annoyance at being questioned clear, and it dawns on me right then.

Perhaps I do not know the right kinds of angels. Perhaps I've always dealt with idiots who believe themselves above everyone else, just like the seraphim. This little rebellious angel is showing me something I've never seen before, and it makes my view of her shift a little.

"You're something else, unicorn," I mumble, unaffected by her threat. "We're going to the building right up there, on the right."

She follows my finger as I point, her eyes finding the neon lights above the place. Her brows rise. "We're going to the Hell Hole?"

"The librarian thinks he's a comedian," I answer, shaking my head. "I've told him it's not funny."

She tilts her head. "It's a little funny."

I roll my eyes. "Not you too. Come on. Let's go in before we have to deal with any more eyes on us. Some of them are looking at me like they'd risk it all for a taste of my hellfire."

"Some of them will welcome it," she muses, glancing over at a woman barely coherent enough to hold her body up. She's filled with drugs of some kind that are so potent, she's no longer in the same world as us. "Some of them will cherish it as they fall to ash."

Those words hang between us. "Would you?" I ask. "Would you welcome it?"

Blue clashes with my black. Her runes flare to life and dance along her skin. Those tempting wings shuffle slightly, just enough to create the sound that makes me want to run my fingers along the feathers.

"It wouldn't be wise."

"Ah, but some of the stupidest decisions turn out to be the best," I murmur, stepping closer. "Why not have a taste of true damnation? After all, you've already been declared an enemy."

Her eyes flash as I move closer, desperate for a taste. "I'm trying to redeem my name."

"Redemption is for humans. Revenge is for sinners like us," I whisper, running a strand of her orange hair across my fingers, feeling the silken smoothness of it. "The fall will be worth it," I promise on a husky breath.

The hottest fires burn blue, and her eyes are no exception. I see the desire flashing there, the urge to give in to me and close the last few shreds of distance between us. I'm not afraid of her fire, of the runes that shine brightly on her skin even here in the darkest of places. You can't burn what's already been scorched, and I've already long since accepted the fire.

"Come on, little angel. Don't you want a taste of hell? Don't you want to dance in the chaos just once?" I purr.

My wings spread wide to block the view behind me, a sign of aggression toward any human that may want to step forward and touch. She sways, and our lips are so close that if I just twitched, they'd be touching. How I long to do so, but I wait, wanting it to be her decision, wanting her to fall by her own free will.

Someone shouts in the distance, and she blinks, the moment interrupted, but she doesn't move away immediately. Her eyes move up from my lips to my eyes. "I always knew the devil would be a gentleman."

I grin. "Unicorn, the devil has got nothing on me."

She blinks again, waking up from whatever trance we'd been in. "I believe you," she murmurs before leaning back, putting distance between us again and looking toward the neon lights. "Let's get this over with."

If I thought I wanted her before, I thought wrong.

The hellfire along my arms reaches toward her as she moves away, wanting to drag her closer, and I startle in surprise. She doesn't notice, thank fuck, but I quickly shove it back into submission.

Still, as she shuffles her wings, small tendrils reach for her, as if the very fires of Soleil have already accepted her.

As if they have already welcomed her home.

CHAPTER 11
ROUX

The Hell Hole is exactly that, a hell hole.

The doors are blown wide open, letting anyone in. Congregated in the reception are those who are down on their luck, their attire clearly revealing just what ailments they have suffered. They eye us as we walk through, taking in our wings and the strangeness of an angel walking side by side with a demon. I ignore the broken elevator and head to the stairs, preferring not to have my wings trapped in a death box anyway. I can feel his eyes on my ass as I walk before him, and when I realize I'm swaying my hips to tempt him, I stop. I feel his chuckle dance across my skin like he knows my thoughts.

I almost kissed him.

Demons are tricky creatures, and it seems the crown prince is intent on stealing my soul. I almost gave in. That fire could burn me up, and I would have welcomed it. No, he's dangerous, especially as desire still pounds through me, stronger than any I've ever felt, keeping my runes alight—which is good since the hallway is dark when we reach the top floor. Once there, he passes me, and I follow silently, still pondering what happened back there. I'm surprised he's not making jokes or needling me, but I'm glad he's not.

However, when he glances over his shoulder to check that I'm still here, there is a very serious look in his eyes that almost makes me stumble. To cover it, I smile. "I wasn't looking at your ass, if you were wondering."

He barks out a laugh and wiggles it. "Sure you weren't, unicorn." He stops before a door and eyes me. "Oh, did I forgot to tell you the librarian hates angels?" He pounds on the door, leaving me cursing as the door rips open from the inside.

A bleary-eyed man holding a bottle of tequila stands there. His lips are twisted in irritation, his brown hair is pushed back, and his glasses are perched on his nose. I don't know what I expected, but it wasn't a troll. His skin is tinted light green, so maybe he's a half breed. They are known for their violence and fighting skills, not knowledge. Oh, and he's right, they hate angels. It might have something to do with angels using them as cannon fodder in war.

"Nope," he says before he slams the door in our faces.

"Charming," I mutter.

"I'll get you hell nectar," the demon beside me calls, and the door rips open again. The troll sticks his head out, and they eye each other with distrust.

"No, she ain't coming in here. All of her kind are fucking annoying."

I gape as he crosses his arms and glares at me.

"I know. She truly is, but we are working together, for now," Vetris placates.

I glance between them and huff.

"He's working with me," I snap as I step toward him, plucking the tequila out of his hand and downing some. It doesn't touch me like angel dust or ambrosia does, but the burn is familiar and good. "And it's been a very bad week, so may we come in?" I ask sweetly.

He eyes me and his bottle. "You owe me another one. I don't want angel germs." He stomps back inside.

"Lovely." I throw back the bottle and drop it inside the door as I step inside and stare at the room in surprise.

There are books and scrolls everywhere—I mean everywhere—piled to the ceiling. The room is the size of a ballroom. It has to be magic. The ceilings are so tall I cannot even see them, yet stacks of books reach for them in piles like a maze, cluttering the room everywhere I look. I have to duck around piles, trying to find the grumpy troll who disappeared within.

"Great, he's a hoarder."

"He prefers collector." The demon chuckles in my ear as he hauls me around some stacks and then flops onto a partially covered couch. He crosses his legs when the librarian appears, another bottle in hand. Ignoring me, the librarian sits and starts to drink, his eyes on the demon.

"What the fuck do you want? Last time I saw you, you got me arrested."

"A misunderstanding." Vetris grins. "We need your help."

"No shit, it's not like you come for the company," the man sneers and finally looks at me. "I don't like her."

The demon chuckles. "Not many people do, it seems."

Leaning forward, I duck my head to catch his eyes. "What do you know of the orb from our world?"

"Straight to the point. Fine, I like that." He leans back, watching me. "Why?"

"None of your business," I snap.

"Then I cannot help you." He shrugs, and I want to smack that tequila bottle over his head. Like he knows my thoughts, Vetris plucks it away and hides it.

"She's got some anger issues, this one," he whispers to the librarian like I can't hear him.

"I do with annoying demons, so keep talking," I retort, and he winks at me.

"Why? Do you like it when we fight?" he purrs.

Throwing my hands up, I go to leave when the librarian huffs.

"Fine. If it will make you leave faster, I'll help, but I want ten years' worth of nectar, not that measly stuff you sent last time."

"Which was five years' worth, and it was gone in one." The demon grins. "But deal."

"Fine, that orb is an ancient spelled object created to maintain balance in your world." He spews out the facts like he knows every magical item in the world. Maybe he does. He stands as he talks, selecting a scroll at random and tossing it to the demon. "Without it, it will be chaos. Celestia will struggle, as will Soleil. Your magic will be out of whack, and it will be chaos. It was created to keep the truce between your two races. Now why do you want to know about it?"

"Oh, because someone stole it, and they think she did." Vetris grins as he thrusts his thumb at me before unrolling the scroll. There's a diagram of an orb and some words scrolled around it, but he rolls it back up before I can get a good look at it.

"Dumb move, angel," the librarian grumbles.

"I didn't steal it!" I yell. "But someone did, and we need to find out who and quickly return it before our world fails."

"So dramatic." The demon groans as he stands. "Fine, come on. I know better than to argue. You'll just get all indignant and angelic on me."

Rolling my eyes, I stand and glare at the librarian. "I would say thank you, but you weren't very helpful."

He toasts me with his new bottle. "Feeling is mutual, angel. Don't let the door hit your perky ass on the way out."

Stomping out of the room in annoyance, I mutter under my breath about idiot trolls as I hit the hallway.

"It really is perky. It was a compliment."

I whirl on the demon behind me, and he grins. Breathing deeply, I try not to rise to the bait. Instead, I head to the door at the end labeled roof.

"Where ya going, unicorn?" he calls after me.

"To save our world, demon," I snarl.

“You’re much more fun when you’re craving cock,” he remarks as I break out onto the roof, the city stretched before us.

“I’ll still kill you,” I threaten as I step up onto the ledge, knowing we have no time to wait.

“You’ll try, and it will end up with us fucking. I can’t wait.” Heading across the roof, he hops up next to me with a grin stretched across his handsome face. “Well then, unicorn, let’s fly.” He leaps off the roof with a finesse that no demon should possess.

“Asshole,” I mutter as I take off into the air after him.

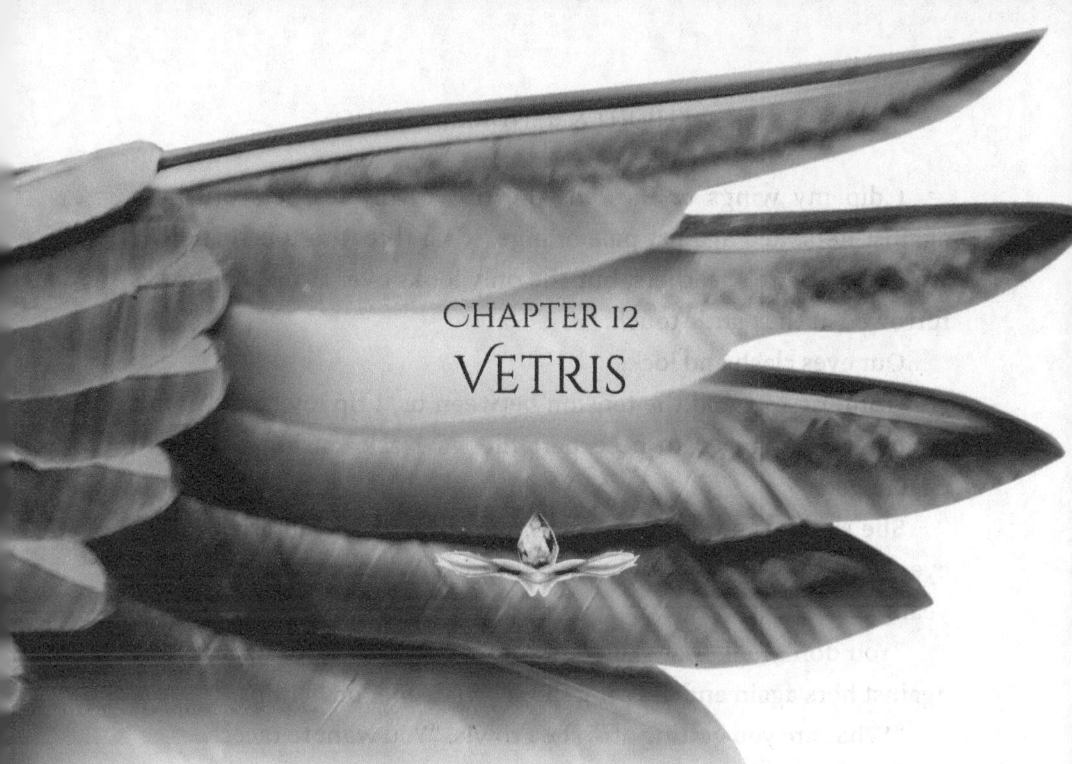

CHAPTER 12
VETRIS

It's been so long since I've been able to spread my wings and fly without worry. Here on Earth, it's not a sign of war as it would be in Soleil. It's just a part of life now. The wind rushes beneath my wings, making everything inside me yearn to show off for the angel flying beside me, even if I know she's likely a skilled flier.

I glance to the side, taking in the glittering beauty that is Roux, the rebellious angel desperate to be seen as the perfect archangel. Despite the clear rebellion in her soul, despite the clear desire to be free, she fights to be accepted right back into the fold and to give up the freedom she currently has. I don't blame her for that. The brainwashing the seraphim encourage is as effective as my own is in Soleil.

There's only one big difference.

Even demons have more freedom than the angels.

But Roux? Roux would be a sight to behold if she decided to forget her mission and stayed on Earth. An angel as bright as her would be famous here. Will she be so bright, though, once she falls and gives in to the desire between us?

I dip my wings to the left, the tips of my feathers brushing against hers. Red against pale orange. It's a threat to touch another winged creature's feathers, but she only looks over at me, her brows furrowed at the gentle touch.

Our eyes clash and lock.

Grinning to avoid the tension between us, I tip my chin. "Aren't archangels supposed to be expert fliers?" I ask, raising a brow in challenge.

She snorts, and I still see her annoyance at the librarian in her eyes, but it's clear the flight is easing it. "Warriors are trained for years, yes."

"You don't look that skilled to me," I goad, my feathers brushing against hers again and drawing the scowl deeper on her lips.

"What are you getting at?" she growls. "You want to race?"

"You'd lose," I point out. "I'm a crown prince, and you're just a lowly little archangel." I don't actually know if I'm faster than her, but it's logical that I would be. I've had centuries to perfect my flying. Roux, in contrast, has had far less time, and even less years as an archangel.

She doesn't rise to my bait, but her brow rises, telling me I might be underestimating her. "What do I get if I win?"

"What would you ask of me?" I catch a wind current and glide along it, watching as she does the same. What a strange sight we probably make to those below, a demon and an angel flying together.

The annoyance disappears from her eyes completely, and something about the sparkle in her eyes makes me want to kiss her or fuck her here, right in the sky, to see if they would sparkle like that while I'm balls deep in her.

"If I win, I get to call you princess."

I narrow my eyes. "No."

"Then the deal's off." She laughs. "I thought you said you were guaranteed to win?"

She's right. I did say that. Fuck. "Fine," I growl. "But if I win, I get to kiss that smug look off your face."

Her grin widens. "Deal."

Fuck. Fuck, fuck, fuck. She's far too confident. While it should piss me off, instead it stokes excitement inside me. A challenge. I haven't had such a challenge in so long.

She looks down at the city beneath us, the skyrises moving around us with our leisurely pace. "We race to the top of the tallest building there." She points to the building. "First one to touch their palm to the door wins."

I nod and pull my wings up to hover in the air. When she does the same, I take in the way her hair blows around her in the wind, how her eyes glitter, and the way her runes flash along her arms. This is the beauty angels should be known for, this fire. Not the bullshit stoic attitude the seraphim demand that forces the fire away. I want to dance with Roux in the sky and to fuck her in the air for the whole city to see.

I want them to witness her fall.

"Ready," she says, her lips curving up. "Set."

"Go!" I growl and shoot toward the building.

I'm motivated to win. I've imagined kissing her lush lips for days now, and I want to so badly, I'm sure my cock would explode at the first touch. My wings flap, their wingspan pushing me through the air without much need for all of the muscle mass beneath the feathers—until Roux shoots past me on wings built for speed, her form perfect, her wings efficient, and I realize just how much trouble I'm in.

"Come on, princess," she teases as she flies right past me. "Surely you can't be giving up already."

A growl tumbles out of my throat before I push myself faster, my large cumbersome wings pushing so much air, I should easily be winning. Still, Roux stays stubbornly just ahead of me, her speed equal to my own, but she'd gotten a head start on me thanks to my underestimation.

She flies just in front of me, arrowing toward the building. We're coming in fast, far too fast, but neither one of us will be hurt too badly as long as we keep our wings spread. I'm sure Roux has been taught the proper ways to land in a hurry. All archangels are true warriors, but I forget the force she actually is because Roux looks the way she does.

The city lights glitter off her wings. A bit of angel dust trails from her feathers and enters the air. Some of it gets in my mouth, my cock immediately reacts, and I want to lick the dust from her skin.

I flap my wings harder, closing the distance between us, but it won't be enough. The building rises before us, too close, and Roux laughs as she flares her wings and tips up. Her feet touch the surface of the roof, forcing her to take quick steps to the door with her speed. I'm right behind her, her hair swirling around her at the force of my own wings. She reaches her palm out just as I reach out mine.

Her palm touches the door and the finish line a millisecond before mine does, but I'm going too fast. As she slams into the door, laughing, I slam around her, my arms bending the door in as I use them to brace myself and keep from crushing her. My wings slam against the walls on either side of the door, and my body presses against Roux's back. Her laughter immediately stops as my warmth surrounds us and my arousal presses against her ass.

I'm panting with desire, with need, but I don't move. If I move, I'm going to fuck her right here against the door.

She shifts, just barely, and I groan at the feeling of her jeans brushing against my erection.

"Don't move," I growl, desperation in my voice. "Just give me a second."

She glances over her shoulder and meets my eyes, her cheeks flushed with her own desire. "You have angel dust on your face," she whispers.

"I know," I snarl, closing my eyes for a moment as I try to come to my senses.

"I can help—"

"Unless you're willing to take off those jeans and let me spear your sweet cunt, leave it alone, unicorn," I rasp, trying to rein in my desire. I take deep breaths, forcing air into my lungs.

She doesn't look away from my face. Those bright blue eyes make me want to steal her away to Soleil, to claim her, and that thought scares me. What the actual fuck? She's the enemy. I'm the crown prince. This is all fucking stupid. I've lost my mind.

"Vetris," she whispers, and I focus on her again, my desire swirling beneath my skin. The hellfire trails along my arms and brushes against her skin. I'm not sure if she even notices, but the flush on her cheeks tells me she's just as turned on as I am.

"You won," I point out, struggling to make myself move, but damn if I don't like the heat of her pressed against me.

She smiles. "Guess I get to call you princess anytime I want."

Leaning back, she closes the distance between us. I'm confused for a moment, not sure what's happening, until she gets a little closer and her gaze falls to my lips. Fuck. I can't do this. If I kiss her, I'm going to lose all control, but demons always walk on the dangerous side.

My eyes fall to her runes, to the way they dance and sparkle, and I'm about to throw all caution to the wind and fucking take her. I don't even care if she beats me to a pulp. I want to kiss her so badly, I'd gladly take some pain for the experience.

I growl, "Unicorn," in warning, but as it turns out, the warning shouldn't have come from me.

Before I can lean in and claim her lips, before I can get my first taste of heaven, angelic power strikes the wall beside us, barely missing my wing as it explodes outward, peppering us with stone and bits of metal.

I whirl, searching for the source, and come face-to-face with a small platoon of angels.

"Your friends are here," I growl, turning to face them completely, my wings spread wide in a show of force. The hellfire dances along my arms, claws along my shoulders, and forms a crown atop my head. A few of the angels blink in surprise, but they don't back down.

I'd been seconds away from tempting my angel to fall, and these assholes interrupted.

They are going to pay for that audacity.

Angel feathers will rain down on the city tonight.

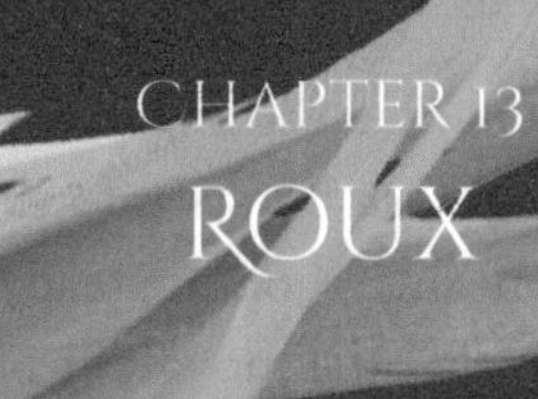

CHAPTER 13
ROUX

Shit, I should have known they would come here and track me themselves.

I was so distracted by my race with Vetris, I didn't even notice them, and for a moment, my cheeks heat, wondering what they saw. Did they see how I was about to kiss him? To give into this desire between us?

I could blame the adrenaline from the race, but it's so much simpler.

I want the crown prince badly.

He stands next to me, irritation and anger pouring off him in waves. It's clear Vetris feels the same. We stand together, wing to wing, facing off with the angels.

"Don't kill them," I mutter.

His head jerks around, flashing me a cocky grin. "No promises, unicorn."

I grasp his arm, ignoring the gasps of the other angels watching. "I mean it. You can't. If you do, I will never be welcomed back. I will be shunned."

"They expect demons to kill them, unicorn," he growls, but I just stare at him. "Fuck. Fine. I'll knock them out, and we can wipe their memories. Happy?"

"Very," I reply as I look back at the angels. "Ready to rock?"

"Baby, I was born ready." He bursts into the air, as if he wasn't just about to fuck me on this roof. Instead, he's now arrowing toward the angels above us. Some move out of his way, but others don't have time with his speed, and they tumble through the sky as he laughs.

Taking to the air, I hesitate for a moment. After all, these are my people, but then an archangel flies closer, sneering at me. Her words carry on the air. "Demon slut."

I stop hesitating.

I might have hit her harder than I meant to. My fist slams into her face, and she tumbles down, blinking incredulously. I let out a very un-angelic snarl as a sword tries to cut through my wings. The flames would singe them and ruin them forever, yet the archangel dared to use it on me. I manage to duck and weave around, slamming my foot into the angel's hand. As the sword falls from his failing grip, I grab it, turning to slam the pommel into his face over and over until he's unconscious. I throw him onto the roof of the building to deal with once I've taken care of the others.

The female comes at me again. I spot the cut healing across her cheek as she arrows herself toward me. We slam back into the building, but I kick her off me. Her wings spread to catch the air and stop her momentum, but I'm already heading straight for her. I wrap my wings around us as we tumble, letting us fall as I slam my fist into her face again. Sneering, she tries to fight me off, but I'm too strong, and when I hit her again, she goes limp in my grip. Spreading my wings, I catch the air and swoop with her in my grip, dropping her next to the other unconscious angel with a thump.

Glancing over, I see Vetris laughing as he fights off four archangels, his wings alight with fire. He's clearly enjoying himself.

Three more are watching from the side, and when they realize I have won my fights, they head my way, surrounding me. They are patient and cold, and I know I won't win this by luck.

Flipping the sword in my grasp as I watch them, I give them a smile. "I don't suppose I can tempt you to fly away?"

"You will pay for your crimes, traitor," one spits.

"Guess not." I sigh. "Okay then, let's do this."

I know we are a blur as we crash together. I use my size to my advantage. I duck under their swords while bringing my own up. One chops the tip off, and I glare before slamming the sword into his face, watching him fall to the city below.

One down, two to go.

They circle me, coming at me from both sides, but I'm stronger and faster. I also have less to lose.

It makes me unpredictable and wild, and when our swords cross above my head, I slam mine into his, making him stagger. I press the advantage, driving him back to the building and then slamming my wings into him. The power and the force knock him out cold. The other catches me with a fist and sends me spiraling below, but I quickly right myself and shoot up until we tangle in the air. Both of us fight for control, for the win. My runes light up under my skin, and before he can break away, I grip him tighter, digging my fingernails in, and then I let my power flow through me.

My power slams into him like a Mac truck. He screams as it burns him, lighting up his own runes until his eyes roll back in his head. I catch him and dump him on the roof. Landing next to the bodies, I quickly touch their foreheads, wiping their immediate memories. It won't touch their long-term memories, but they will forget seeing us. When Vetris plops five more down, all wiped, I grin at him.

"Time to go, princess." I push off of the roof and into the air, knowing he'll follow.

Things just got a whole lot more complicated, and I don't just mean between us.

~

DABBING the wound on his cheek, I ignore his heated gaze as he watches me work. We are perched on top of a bridge high in the sky, the clouds surrounding us cutting off the world below. "I can't believe you let them land a blow, princess," I tease.

"I got distracted by your ass," he admits, making me grin and shake my head. His hand catches my arm as I wipe at his small wound, making me still as my eyes jerk up to his. We are inches apart and so close I can feel his heat and see the lust firing in his eyes.

Post battle sex is incredible, but I refuse to give in with him.

I can't.

"You don't have to feel guilty about wanting me, unicorn." It's not what I expected him to say, and I recoil a little. "You think you would be the first angel to fuck a demon?" His head cocks to the side, and when I just stare, he sighs. "You really do, don't you? What do they teach you up there? Clearly they hide the truth."

"What truth?" I demand.

"Angels and demons, we might be enemies, little angel, but that doesn't stop us from mating. Couples throughout history have chosen each other and left both sides."

"That's not true," I argue, jerking my hand out of his grasp and dropping the bloody cloth I had been using. "It can't be."

"Of course it is. They have lied to you. Mating, though not common, has happened between our races throughout the past, and even if it doesn't end in a forever mating, angels and demons like to... enjoy each other." He runs his tongue over his teeth as he says that.

"Have you?"

"Jealous?" He grins, and when I glare, he chuckles. "I've never had an angel, never wanted to, but you are changing that."

"Enough. This is a lie." I go to stand, but he yanks me back down, making me still as he cups the back of my head so we are almost pressed nose to nose.

"I have no reason to lie to you," he murmurs.

"To spread chaos? To make me give in? To hurt the angels?" I snap. "Take your pick."

"Fine, I have reason, but it's the truth, unicorn. I'm thousands of years old. I lived through the war and have watched our races over the years. I've seen it all. Your people are lying to you, Roux. They want us even as much as they hate us."

Struggling, I try to pull away, but he keeps me close, the strength in his body making me still once more. "Why?" I croak. "Why are you telling me?"

"So that when I do this, you don't get all holy and guilty on me." He slams his lips onto mine.

I'm frozen against him, right and wrong tangling in my mind. My desire and my duty war until finally, my desire gives in. Anger surges through me at my own needs, at him kissing me, at him tempting me, until I grip his hair and kiss him right back.

It's an angry kiss, full of clashing teeth and tongues. I swallow his groan as I yank on his hair until it hurts, and in return, his hand slides around my throat, pinning me to him.

This kiss shocks me to my very soul, as if hellfire is sliding through my veins and into my heart and soul, rebranding it. I moan into his lips as his hand tightens on my throat, his tongue tangling with mine as we both fight for control. A storm of lust, hate, and adrenaline pours through us both.

But then reality comes crashing down.

We break apart, both of us breathing heavily as we stare at each other. "We shouldn't have done that," I finally force out, my voice breathy with desire.

"I agree. Let's do it again." His head swoops in, and I jerk away, falling off the side of the bridge before I let my wings spread out to catch me. "Well, that's a first—a woman actually falling and almost dying to avoid my kiss." He rubs at his head as he watches me.

"That never happened," I snap. "Ever. Now let's get going. We have an orb to find."

Swinging his legs over the side, he watches me carefully. "Pretend all you want, unicorn, but we both know you'll give in, and I'm done fighting it. I will have you, angel, and it will be so sweet to watch you fall."

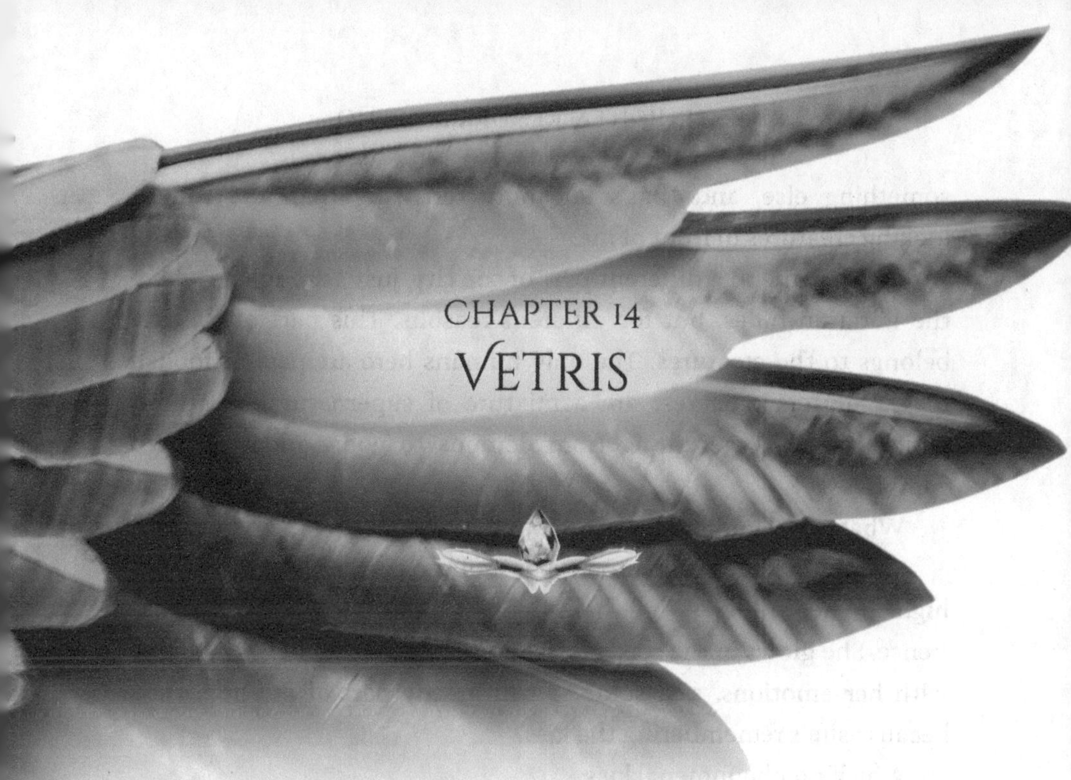

CHAPTER 14
VETRIS

Something is wrong.

I haven't felt this… incandescent in centuries. I try to blame it on the hunt, on this adventure, and everything happening around me. I even try to blame it on being able to fly unrestricted through the skies. Maybe it was the fight with the angels, since it's been so long since I've had a good fight. But I recognize all of that for the lies they are.

This feeling is because of the angel at my side.

Hatred. That's all.

I hate the angels and everything they pretend to stand for, their brainwashing and indoctrination, and their holier than thou attitudes. The angels are nothing but prudish assholes willing to kill their own than own up to whatever bullshit they have going on. Roux clearly didn't take the orb. From everything I've seen, she's exactly what an angel should be—strong, caring, bold, and brilliant.

Fuck.

It's not hatred. It's not hatred at all. Yes, I still hate the angels, especially the seraphim, but Roux? I don't hate her at all. This is something else, and that's far more terrifying than the rough-looking creatures in front of me.

We've come to a different part of the city, just as rough as where the librarian hides, but for different reasons. This part of the city belongs to the creatures. The only humans here are pets or foolish magic chasers. The rest are a mixture of supernatural creatures, which includes everything from demons to gods, and wolves to vampires.

Whatever your kink is, you can find it here.

Watching Roux walk into this part of the city, with her chin held high and her brilliant wings held tightly against her back, is an experience. She glows in the seedy darkness. The runes on her skin flicker with her emotions, and some selfish greedy part of me hopes it's because she's remembering the kiss.

A fucking phenomenal kiss.

Is kissing all angels like that? Or is it just this particular angel? At my thought, the hellfire along my arms flickers and reaches out toward her, wanting her just as much as I do. That should be a bad sign, but some evil part of me wants to pin her down beneath me, fuck her as she screams my name, and let my hellfire consume her. I want her to be marked with me, to find ecstasy in the fall, and to beg me for damnation.

I want her. Period.

I've never wanted a woman more.

"Vetris?"

I blink and glance over at Roux. She's looking at me with furrowed brows. "What?"

"I asked if this is the right place," she says, clearly repeating something I hadn't heard.

I clear my throat and look in the direction she's pointing, taking in the neon sign of a snake. "Yes, this is it."

She doesn't question where my mind was. She doesn't prod. I take that to mean she likely knows what I'm thinking about, and the slight flush on her cheeks confirms it.

My little angel is thinking about fucking me just the same.

There's a vampire at the door, manning the line. When both of us walk up to the front, he glares. "The line is back there."

I let my hellfire move, and the crown appears on my head. "Try again."

The vampire blinks and bows his head slightly. The vampires aren't beholden to demonic laws, but it would be foolish to treat Soleil's crown prince with anything but respect. "Your Majesty. Please, come in."

Roux raises her brow at me but walks ahead when I gently touch her lower back. We enter the club, the inside pulsing with a deep, sensual beat. The darkness hides some of the more unsavory things going on, but the flashing lights highlight it every now and then. Roux moves a little closer to me when she sees the crowd, uneasy with the sheer number of dangerous creatures, and that gives me pleasure. I keep my hand on the small of her back, a comfort and a promise.

If given the opportunity, I'd take her into one of these dark corners and fuck her right here, let her angel dust rain around me, and send the club into a frenzy.

Roux's eyes trail up to those who are swinging and dancing on silks hanging from the ceiling. Some of them are definitely fucking up there. Even though I can't hear it over the music, I can smell it. I'm sure Roux can too.

We didn't come here to linger though. What I wouldn't give to feed my unicorn some ambrosia and watch her sway to the beat of the music, but we don't have time for that. More angels will hunt her, and eventually they'll realize I have no intention of delivering her to them. The seraphim will get desperate and angry.

I push Roux through the crowd toward the bar on the far side of the room. There's a female there, a powerful one, but I can't get a read on what she is without seeming rude—that is until she looks at me and her eyes swirl with galaxies.

I bow my head, just barely.

"You've come seeking an answer," she says by way of greeting as she dries a glass with a towel. "Ask."

Roux looks between us, confused, but she trusts me and what I'm doing. That shouldn't make something inside me tighten in worry. It's not wise to trust a demon, especially a prince.

"We're looking for an artifact, an orb," I reply, staring into the galaxy of her eyes.

She hums under her breath as she sets the glass down on the counter and picks up another, repeating the action. Those galaxies flash once, twice, before she sets down the glass and leans in.

"The item you seek is hidden in plain sight, princeling."

"Where?" I ask, the hair on my arms standing on end. This creature, this otherworldly creature, unnerves me.

"Home," she murmurs before leaning back. "Now get out of my club."

I nod and pull Roux away. "Wait," Roux says. "What does that mean?"

Despite the music, I hear her question loud and clear. "We're returning to Soleil, unicorn. That's what it means."

"You owe me money for the cleanup," the woman behind the bar grumbles, and I glance at her in confusion.

"I'm sorry, what?"

Before she can answer, a demon comes stumbling through the crowd, a bottle of something thick in his hand. He reeks of stale cigarettes and old sex, and it makes me wrinkle my nose. He stops before Roux, his dark eyes taking in her glow. Too many are looking at her and the way she gives off light. They are drawn to it, as all dark creatures are drawn to the light.

"So pretty," the demon growls. "Are you looking for a good time, pretty angel?"

"No, thank you," Roux says primly, which should have been the end of that. He asked, and she answered.

The demon sneers at her answer and lurches forward, his fingers suddenly grabbing her wrist. "Look here, bitch. This isn't Celestia, so you're going to kneel and take my co—"

I see red. That's the only way I can describe it. It starts off red and spreads to blue, my anger a fierce thing I can't control. One moment, I'm watching this lower demon grab Roux. The next, the music cuts off abruptly as his head thumps to the floor, dead. Roux stumbles back in surprise, a few drops of black blood splattering her skin. How dare he touch her even in death?

The creatures around us are silent as I stand there, hellfire dancing along my shoulders, before their eyes drift over to the bartender with galaxy eyes. She doesn't react, still cleaning that fucking glass.

"That's why you owe me for cleanup," she says, unfazed.

Just like that, the music starts up again, and the club returns to normal. The watcher has spoken.

"Come on. Let's get out of here," I grumble, gently pushing Roux toward the exit.

"What was that about?" she asks, her eyes on me.

"Leave it," I growl, but I don't have an answer.

I just killed one of my own kind for her, all because he dared to touch her, call her a bitch, and threaten her. She's an archangel. She doesn't need my protection, but regardless, I gave it.

Why? What is this draw I feel toward the angel that I can't fight? It's not hatred or anger. It's something else.

I don't want to look too closely at it. I'm not prepared to, not yet.

We leave the club and step back out onto the dark street.

"We're going back? Are you sure it's a good idea?" she asks, her wings relaxing now that we're no longer in a crowd.

"No, I'm not sure," I rasp, glancing at her. "But the orb is in Soleil. The watcher doesn't lie."

She studies me for a moment, really studies me. Whatever she sees brings a small smile to her lips.

"What will they say when you lead an archangel into the depths of Soleil?" she asks teasingly.

"That I've corrupted you. That I got a new pet," I reply honestly.

She snorts. "Perhaps it is I who has a new pet," she says, a sparkle in her eyes. When I just stare at her, she gestures to the sky. "Shall we go, princess?"

I don't answer. Instead, I spread my wings and take to the air, knowing she's following along behind me, but her words echo in my mind.

Perhaps it is I who has a new pet.

The thought doesn't repulse me. If Roux wanted an attack dog, I would happily be so. If the angels don't stop, I'll gladly tear them to shreds in her honor. What I wouldn't do just to have her kiss me again, just to have her look at me with that smile. I'd burn them all for her, and that thought scares me just as much as it excites me.

We aim south and fly toward Brazil.

Flying home.

CHAPTER 15
ROUX

The trip back through the portal is uneventful. No one even glanced in our direction, and once we hit the wasteland between his world and mine, we hesitate.

I cannot return to Celestia, but hiding in Soleil with him just might be a fate worse than death. Not to mention I would voluntarily be surrounding myself with thousands of my natural enemies. I would have to rely on Vetris, the crown prince, to protect me from his own people, and I don't know if I can. Despite what he did in the club, part of me worries this is all a game and that I'm walking into a trap.

No, it's more than my internal debate that has us hesitating, wing to wing, on the desolate land. It's the wrongness of it and the sense of imbalance in the air. The ground under our feet almost shakes with it. Celestia, high above the clouds, is not only visible, but the edges seem to be crumbling. The usual sunlight is gone, replaced by darkness that seems never ending, the moon along with it.

"Something is wrong," Vetris mumbles.

"I know." I share a glance with him. "Do you think it's the orb?"

Pulling out the scroll, he glances at it. "Maybe. Either way, we should get somewhere safe before we decide on our next move. Come." He holds out his hand, and I hesitate. "Roux?"

"Is it a trap?" I find myself asking as I turn to him. "If I follow you to Soleil, are you going to lock me away, torture me, and use me for entertainment?"

"I plan to use you alright, little unicorn." He smirks before it fades when he sees how worried I am. "Roux, I give you my solemn oath, I will protect you from my kind." He crosses his arms over his chest, a cut appearing on his wrist—a blood oath. It shocks me to my core, and I take his hand. If he promised it like that, it must be true.

But who will protect me from him?

"Maybe I could go back and explain," I start as he turns us and begins walking.

"They will imprison you right away," he scoffs. "You know what I say is true, unicorn. This is the only way."

"To Soleil it is then." I sigh, glancing up at Celesta, missing the open skies, the sun on my wings, the clash of swords, and the nectar of angels, but when I look down to find Vetris watching me with something akin to longing in his eyes, I realize I don't miss it all that much.

In fact, I hadn't thought about it once while I was with him.

Hand in hand, we take to the sky, staying low to avoid the angels' detection, and after an hour or so of flying, we stop above a giant crater. Deep below, I see fires burning in the darkness, and Vetris glances at me with a knowing grin. His eyes sparkle as hellfire dances across his skin, igniting the crown atop his head.

"Ready to descend to hell, angel?"

"As ready as I'll ever be," I admit, and then he pulls me over the edge, and we free-fall below.

~

It is not what I imagined.

Vetris stops our descent just above a patch of fire-red grass on top of a hill and lands us on our feet. He releases my hand as I step forward to take in Soleil spread out before me.

It is nothing like I expected.

There are cobbled streets spreading throughout the city like a network. They seem to be separated into zones for different types of demons, like we do angels. Some are smaller, some are taller, and some seem to go underground or even upside down, but all are well kept, in shades of dark browns and blacks, but still beautiful. There are shops and restaurants, and demons walk, talk, and shop before us, not sparing us a look. It's a community. I expected chaos, but this is just like Celestia, only with demons. I guess we aren't so different after all.

The only thing that is exactly how I imagined it would be is a giant, sprawling black castle at the very back of Soleil. It's built into the rocks, which light up with fire. The palace is huge, and spikes cover the top, but it's still beautiful in its own way.

"I didn't expect this," I say out loud as I turn to see Vetris watching me.

"What did you think? All flames, torture chambers, and screams?" He chuckles as he takes my hand and leads me into the street.

"Kind of, I guess," I admit with a shy smile as I look back. "This is... nice."

Gasping, Vetris presses a hand to his chest as he walks backwards through the street. "Don't be so kind, unicorn. I might start to think you'll like it here."

"Don't get cocky." I roll my eyes. "Oh wait, you always are."

Stopping, he almost lets me run into him. His arms wrap around me and tug me closer, uncaring about those who stop to watch. Expressions of shock cross their faces, as if they have never seen this before. My face reddens at the attention. "Only with you so close, with the scent of your desire for me filling my nose, unicorn. Now unless you want to give my subjects a show, I suggest we go to the castle, study the scroll, have wicked rough sex, find the orb, and right the world again."

"In that order, huh?" I tease as I push away, even as I'm slightly shaken by the surety that I will give into him.

"Fine, we will have sex first. You're right, we shouldn't wait that long." He turns, whistling as he walks away.

Rolling my eyes, I bite back my curse and follow him, not wanting to be left alone with demons who look like they want to eat my soul for breakfast.

This is going to be interesting.

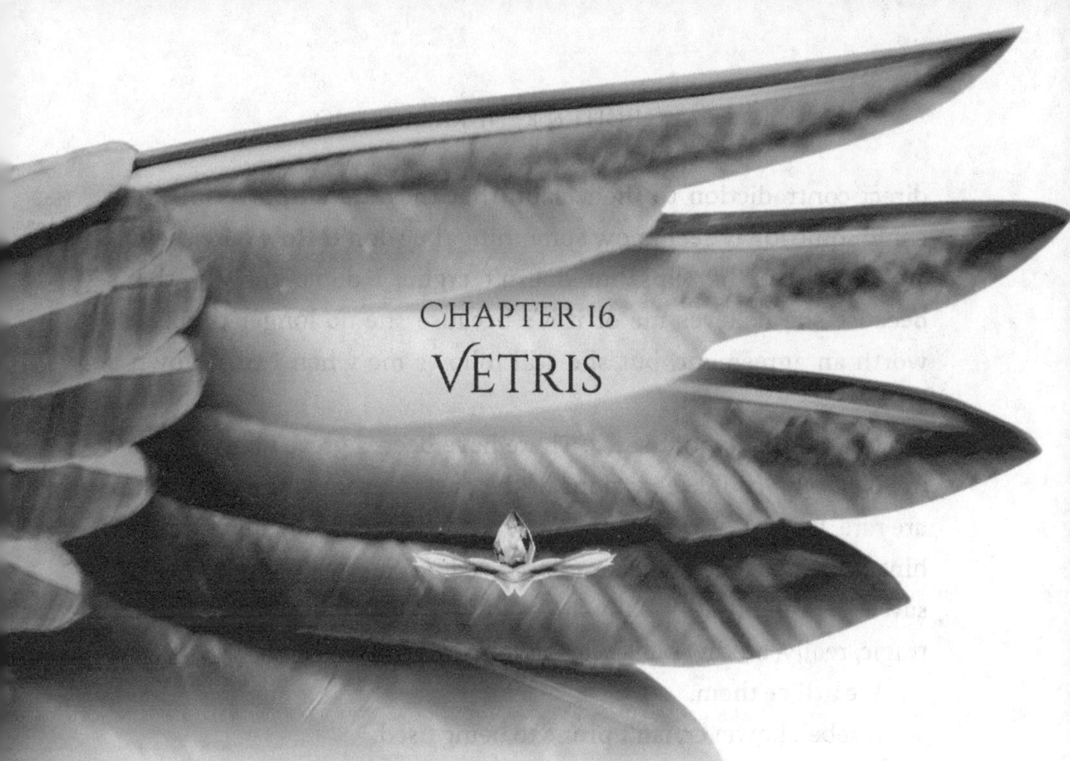

CHAPTER 16
VETRIS

"So what now?" Roux asks, walking by my side. She looks completely at ease despite being thrown into the fire, literally. Hellfire dances along the streets every so often, leading the way toward my castle—as if anyone could miss its location. She could be anxious and nervous, but those aren't words that would ever describe my unicorn. She's a warrior who earned her place as an archangel, so it makes sense that she wouldn't cower despite the situation.

It almost makes me... proud.

Some small part of me wants to treat her like a trophy for all my people to see, while another part, an even smaller part, wants to dangle her in front of the angels like a beacon while I yell, *Look what I'm corrupting. Look what you pushed toward me. Look who likes a little bit of hellfire.*

"There's a seer in—"

"A seer?" Roux interrupts. "Seers don't exist."

"Perhaps not in Celestia, but they do here." I shrug. "Your precious seraphim don't believe in such powers, mostly because it's a direct contradiction to their claim that they are all powerful. How could some lowly seer know something they don't? How dare they?"

She purses her lips but doesn't argue. I don't know if that's because she believes me or if it's because she no longer thinks it's worth an agreement, but she still follows me when I turn down a street.

I hadn't lied about seers. There have been a great many demons in Soleil who could see visions of the past, present, and future. They are rare, but not as rare as angel seers. The moment an angel shows a hint of being a seer, they are destroyed, no matter their age. I once saw a seraphim kill a baby angel for suspecting it had visions. It's tragic, really, but in Soleil, we don't fear seers.

We utilize them.

Jezebel, however, isn't prone to being used.

There is only ever one seer at a time in Soleil. Not because it's not allowed, but because of how they are born. It's as if some higher power only chooses to gift us one a century. Either way, that leaves us with Jezebel, who is a fucking bitch of a seer.

Her home is a quaint little cottage on a street filled with antique stone houses. Where most are dark stone, Jezebel's is pale in color. There's a neon eye on the front door that blinks every so often, signifying what she is. Roux steps forward and stares at the building in surprise.

"I expected a seer to be more... spooky."

I grin at her. "I think you'll find Jezebel lacking in all aspects then."

The door jerks open, and the seer herself walks out dressed completely opposite to what one would expect. I've dealt with many seers in my lifetime, but none like Jezebel. She's wearing brightly colored pants, as if someone threw different paints across them. The flared hems are so wide, she almost looks like a bell. Her top is a simple white shirt that reveals her midriff and the white tattoos that cover her dark skin. There's a fine white line on her forehead in the shape of the same eye on her door. As I stare at it, the tattoo blinks, just like that sign. I'm not surprised by it, but Roux is. I can feel her tension and desire to step back, but she holds strong.

Just as an archangel should.

Jezebel tips her nose up, and when her voice comes, it's with a bitchy undercurrent that always makes my dick want to shrivel into a ball. "Anyone who finds me lacking isn't welcome here. Especially not an angel."

Jezebel's wings arch up, the tendons in the appendages stark against the soft yellow membrane. Her beautiful wings seem misplaced on a demon, but Jezebel has always been a contradiction.

"Not lacking," Roux replies, blinking at the demon. "Just not what I was expecting."

"Ah." Jezebel tsks. "You expected me to wear overly large robes and too much jewelry, and walk around spouting nonsense about impending doom and gloom?" She waves her hands through the air. "Yes, I do that, but only when the situation warrants it. You might even find a crystal ball or two in my home, though those are more for decoration than any usefulness. Come, I've been expecting you." She points at Vetris in accusation. "I've been expecting you for months and you still waited until now."

"I had no reason to come," I say gently, almost fondly. Jezebel, despite her oddity, is still someone I might consider a friend if demons had such things.

"Says you." She sniffs, crossing her arms. "You only come when you need something. How typical of a crown prince. Come off the street. You'll draw more attention the longer you're out here, and attention might eventually get you killed."

Roux tenses. "Is that a vision you had or—"

"It's common sense. A demon and an angel walking side by side, brushing wings intimately, is bound to cause trouble." Jezebel disappears inside, leaving the door open.

Roux glances at me. "She's..."

"Brilliant," I supply. "I know."

"I was going to say interesting, but brilliant works too."

Roux steps forward into an unknown demon's house, unafraid, with her head held high. After a few moments, I follow behind.

This should be interesting.

THE INSIDE of Jezebel's home is as strange as the outside. The room is filled with knick knacks on shelves that are fitting for a seer but still seem strange. To the left is Jezebel's bone collection, a rather diverse display that includes everything from angel wing bones, to a snake taxidermy curling around one of the aforementioned crystal balls, to a small bone from my wing she once won in a rather intense game of poker. When you start offering body parts, you know the game is loaded.

"Don't bother sitting," Jezebel calls from deeper inside the home. "You won't be here for long."

Roux frowns but doesn't sit. Instead, she tucks herself against the wall and waits, her eyes taking in the trinkets on the shelves. She raises her eyebrow. "This is more what I was expecting, to be honest."

Jezebel reappears, carrying a handful of crystals that I don't know the names for, her fingers dancing over them as she tumbles them between her digits. "You have a mission, I'm afraid. There won't be much time for leisure once you figure things out."

I snort. "Do I need to ask the question to make it official, or would you rather we pretend you haven't already seen why we're here?"

Roux looks between the two of us, her eyes brilliant in this light. The orange in her wings is highlighted by the flickering candles placed strategically around the room. Only a fool would think they are just for ambiance. Those candles serve a purpose for Jezebel and nothing more.

At my question, Jezebel grins and walks closer to flick me on the nose. Any other crown prince might have gotten angry, but not me.

Not with Jezebel. We once walked into a battle together and came out alive only because of each other's help. There are no hard feelings between us.

She's a bitch, and I'm an asshole. It works in our friendship.

"Impatient prince today, aren't you?" She grins over at Roux. "Might it be because of a certain—"

"Jezebel," I warn. Now isn't the time for teasing.

"Very well." She scowls at me. "Always taking the fun out of things. Anyways, you're looking for the orb. I don't know where it is."

I bare my teeth, prepared to give her shit for wasting our time, but she holds up her hand to stop me.

"But," she continues, "if you're looking for the answers you seek and the orb, you need to find Abraxos."

I pause. "Abraxos?" When I glance over at Roux, she looks equally as confused. "The old demon who hangs out in the square and holds up a sign saying, 'The end is near?' That Abraxos?"

Jezebel's eyes sparkle. "Shame on you, Vetris, for judging that demon before you've learned anything about him." Her gaze moves over to Roux. "I would have thought you'd learned by now."

Roux shifts under the attention, and a soft blush heats her cheeks. "So we just find this demon and he'll know how to help?" she asks, trying to redirect Jezebel's focus.

Jezebel laughs, her bright eyes hazy with the future and the present. "Just stick close to your mate, archangel, and together, you'll be fine."

Roux's face twists at the same time mine does. She has a mate? After all this time, she's never revealed that? I'm one second away from shutting down and forcing myself to turn away from the angel I so desperately want, but Roux's next words stop me.

"Mate? I don't have a mate," Roux counters, her brows drawn low. She's equally as confused as I am.

Jezebel laughs. "Angels and demons are all the same, never seeing what's right in front of them." She gestures flippantly toward me. "Of course you have a mate. He's standing right there." She starts to laugh at our expressions. "Don't tell me you haven't realized it yet." I open my mouth and close it, not sure what to say. "Oh, wow. I expected better of you, Vetris. Really."

"We need to go," I say, my voice choked.

It makes sense, but I don't want it to. The pull I thought was just hatred and the urge to corrupt this specific angel isn't just hatred at all. How could I have missed it? There is a tugging sensation in my chest, and I feel such an intense need for her.

We're mates.

Holy fuck, we're mates.

Roux's face is distorted in horror, and it brings reality crashing back in.

Demons and angels can't be mates because they are exterminated for it, and even though I'm going to protect Roux with all that I am, I can't force her into that sort of relationship. She wants to go back to Celestia, and a demon like me doesn't belong there.

No. It's impossible. We can't be mates. Jezebel is wrong. She has to be. Roux would never accept such a thing.

I tell myself that over and over despite knowing one single fact—Jezebel, the seer who sees in color, is never, ever wrong.

CHAPTER 17
ROUX

Jezebel, the seer, was... interesting, to say the least.

As we leave her cottage, her laughter following us, I can't help but glance at Vetris to see if his face is twisted like mine is. She called us mates. She has to be wrong. Has to be. I refuse to accept that like I do everything else. I ignore it, but I can't help the stiffness in my wings. It was a lot of information, too much to process, and I can't get the seer's words out of my mind.

"So where do we find Abraxos?" I mutter, trying to get back on track. The quicker we find the orb, the quicker I can go back to Celestia and ignore everything that has happened with the demon prince walking next to me.

"Probably in the square," he mutters distractedly.

Grinding my teeth, I look away, but something else tugs at me, something that started inside of the seer's cute if not cluttered cottage—jealousy, I realize. Watching them interact had only confirmed my fear as soon as he mentioned her. There was fondness there and private knowledge, but seeing it and thinking it were two separate things. They teased, laughed, and smiled, and when he looked at her, his face was soft, not like the angry, masterful look I usually get. He watched her with nothing but admiration, even as they bickered.

Were they lovers once upon a time?

Are they still?

Moreover, why do I care?

He is nothing to me. One stupid kiss doesn't mean anything, and I'm going back to Celestia after this. He can fuck whoever he wants —or so I tell myself, but it doesn't stop the stabbing pain in my chest or the sick feeling in my stomach.

She was really beautiful, and now I start to look around and realize that there are many beautiful demons here, all watching him with desire. They practically throw themselves at his feet as he walks through their midst. He doesn't seem to notice, but I'm no fool.

"What's wrong, unicorn?" His voice snaps me from my thoughts as I glare at a particularly busty demon who bent over for his attention. When I bring my gaze to him, I see frown lines tugging at his forehead. "Is it about what Jez said?"

Fuck.

I need to say something, anything. I don't even want to discuss what—that thing, Jezebel, said.

"You two were very close," I blurt out, and I instantly regret it.

I want to take it back. I want the ground to swallow me whole.

He stops in the middle of the street, his head cocked as he watches me, and he frowns before his expression suddenly morphs into pleasure.

"You're jealous." He grins and barks out a laugh as I glare at him.

Fine, let him believe that. It's easier than discussing the other thing.

The mate thing.

"I am not." I huff, crossing my arms. "It was just a comment. If you don't want to address it, then fine." I start to walk away, uncaring that I don't have a clue where I am going. Anywhere is better than being here with him and those knowing eyes filled with mirth.

"Roux, wait," he calls. I hear him chasing after me, and those around us look on in surprise. When he catches up with me, his hand clamps around my arm, spinning me around until we are practically nose to nose. His wings come up and shield us, giving us privacy, but also cloaking us in darkness—a darkness that is thick with tension. "Jez and I are friends."

"I don't care." I go to duck under his wings, but he grips my arm tightly, tugging me closer until we are plastered together and I can feel the steady if not slightly fast beat of his heart.

"Look into my eyes, feel my heart, and see the truth. We have never been anything more. She is, well, probably one of my only real friends," he tells me, frowning again. "I admit I like your jealousy and possessiveness, little angel, but I don't want you to feel hurt or be angry with me. I vow it to you. We have always been friends and never have been or will be anything more. She is just my friend, unicorn. Believe that."

I risk a glance at his dark eyes, and a vise I didn't know was wrapped around my heart releases, making me gulp in air as if I hadn't been able to breathe. His hand strokes across my arm as he watches me and the myriad of emotions that dance across my face.

"Okay," I mutter.

"Okay?" he repeats, smiling again. "Is this almost a truce, unicorn?"

"Shut up," I mutter reflexively.

"Make me," he demands, his eyes darkening as his tongue darts out to lick his lips. I follow the movement. Desire bursts to life within me despite where we are. I feel his heart speed up and his body heat against mine.

I nearly shake with the need to touch him and taste him and place my mark on him so no other will again...

I'm practically panting as my eyes dart to his lips and back to his gaze, which dances with flames of hunger. "Do you want me to kiss it all better, angel?" he purrs, seduction rolling off him in waves as I lean into him.

Our desire is a living, breathing entity both of us are fighting, yet it only pulls us closer.

Hidden in his wings, I could just reach up and press my lips against his.

He would take over, and I could blame him after, getting what I want now.

No, that's wrong.

I stumble back, breaking the spell, and quickly duck under his wings. My heart is racing, and my skin is flushed and bright with my markings reacting to my emotions. I feel frazzled and embarrassed, but when I look over, he's not faring any better. His eyes are bright with want as he tracks me, his hair is mussed from my hand, and his wings almost tremble with need.

No, we are both just as lost, and we are both fighting this just as hard.

ABRAXOS ISN'T in the square.

"Is there anywhere else he could be?" I demand, my hands on my hips as I glare at the square as if that will make him appear.

"In a hurry?" Vetris jokes. "Want to get out of Soleil as quickly as possible?"

"Something like that," I respond. He doesn't have to know it's to get away from him before I give into this thing between us.

"He has to have a house," I continue as I turn, looking over the square. "Where is it?"

"Not a clue." He shrugs like he doesn't have a care in the world.

"Well, you can track him—"

"I don't have anything of his to track him with," he interrupts, countering my every argument.

"Fine, what do you suggest, demon?" I hiss.

Smirking, he pushes off the wall he was leaning against and doesn't stop until he stands before me, lowering his head. For a moment, I think he's going to kiss me, and I brace myself, but he swerves at the last second and his lips caress my ear. "We get a drink." He steps back and walks away, whistling as if he doesn't have a care in the world.

I gape after him.

With no other choice, I follow. The swinging black door of a bar almost hits me as I rush to keep up, but when I step inside, he's gone. It's crowded with an array of different demons, who all turn to gawk at me. To the right is a long bar lit from within with fire, with bottles of sparkling liquids on top of it. Some tables float in the air with demons sitting at them, while some are buried in holes in the ground. I scan the masses until I spot Vetris at one in the back and, ignoring the looks, head his way. I plop down on the red velvet chair opposite him and cross my arms.

"What the fuck are we doing here, princess?" I demand.

The noise slowly starts back up again as a goblet appears before Vetris. Eyes on me, he sips it.

"Vetris," I warn, but just then, a pink-haired demon with nothing but a G-string on bounces over. Her bare tits sway with the movement, and two chains rattle between them, linked to piercings in her nipples. She leans over Vetris and practically shoves them in his face.

"My prince," she purrs. "Want some company?"

Motherfucker.

Some irrational part of me wants to kill her, my hands fisting under the table. Instead, I settle for a verbal attack, not wanting to start a war in here. I would win, but I don't think Vetris would be happy if I killed his people.

"Fuck off," I snap at the demon. She turns her glare on me. "We are busy."

Vetris leans back in his chair, grinning as he dangles a goblet from one hand. His eyes are only for me, and they are bright with happiness.

"You dare to speak to me like that, angel?" she roars, reaching for me as if she's about to attack, but her crown prince speaks, stopping her.

"I wouldn't do that if I were you, demonling." He winks at me, not even bothering to look at her, and for some reason, that pleases me more than I can explain. "My girl here is an archangel and can kick your ass without breaking a sweat. Isn't that right, unicorn? Either way, she's right, we are busy, so scurry away." He waves her off, and with a glare at me, she tosses her hair and bounces away.

I watch her go with a narrow-eyed look, and when I glance back at Vetris, he leans over the table, grips the back of my neck, and tugs me until his lips meet my skin.

"I love it when you get all possessive, angel. Want to ride me here so they all know I'm yours?" he taunts.

"What are we doing here?" I snarl, repeating my other question now that the demon is gone. I try to ignore the flush on my cheeks as I imagine taking him here in this booth and marking him as mine. Temptation flutters in my chest.

He just chuckles, not the least bit put off as he leans back once more, relaxing like he doesn't have a care in the world. "One of Abraxos's buddies comes here every night. We are waiting for him to arrive. Ah, speak of the… There he is."

Downing his drink, he stands and pulls me up. His fingers link with mine to keep me with him as he winds through the bar. I like his touch way too much and should really shake his hand off. I can follow without being led like a child, but instead, I keep my fingers firmly in his.

"Where's Abraxos?" Vetris demands as soon as he reaches the easily nine-foot demon he saw from across the bar.

"What do I look like? His keeper?" he growls, but then he turns and sees who is behind him. "Shit, sorry, my prince." He bows, practically scraping the floor with how low he goes. "He resides up top, between the two lands. He has a house there. I can take you."

Without another word, Vetris tugs me out of the bar and back into the bustling center of Soleil, not even letting the demon finish.

It's only when we get back onto the street that I realize I'm still holding his hand… and I don't let go.

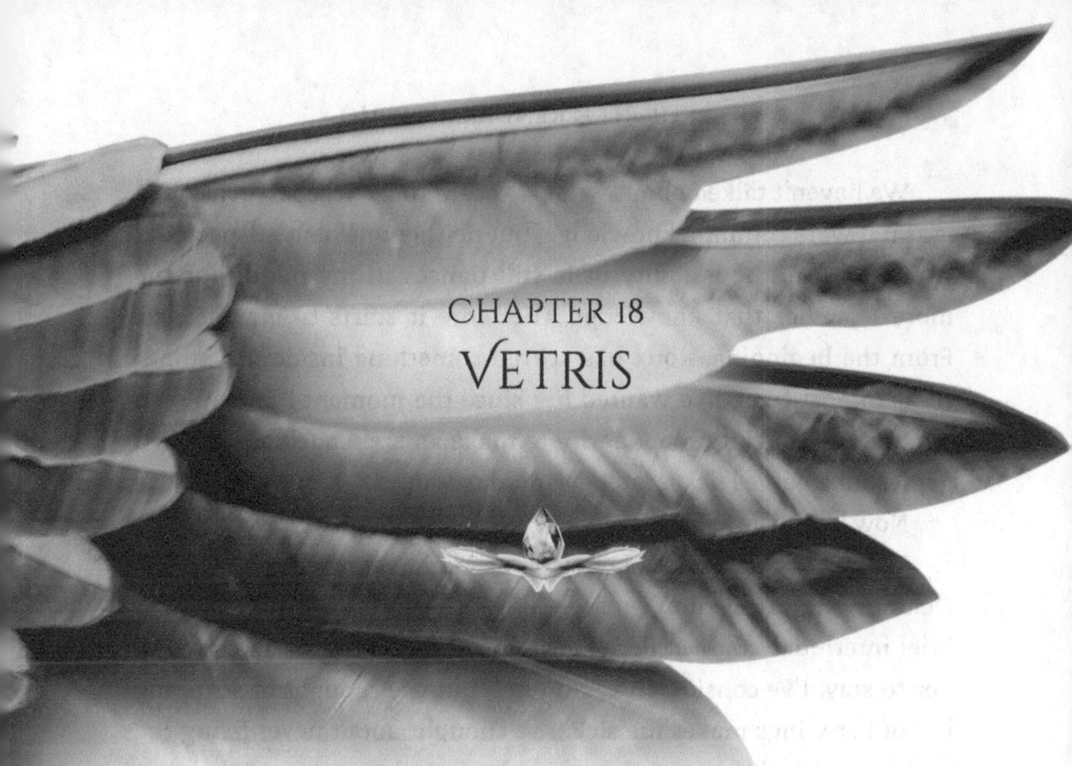

CHAPTER 18
VETRIS

I remember when the wastelands used to be green and thriving. Before the war between Celestia and Soleil, the in-between was a place of neutrality, where demons and angels could go about their business unscathed. Sure, there were fights, but those were easily dealt with. It takes me a few long seconds to recall what it used to look like before the war began so long ago, but when Roux and I step foot up top again, that vision is wiped away by what's left in this era.

Barrenness. Death. Decay.

Where there was once lush green vegetation, there's only dried up husks of what once was. Remnants of trees and plant life dot the landscape, and the ground is cracked and dry to the point that if it were to somehow come back to life, the resulting floods would be catastrophic for Soleil. I doubt the seraphim care about the demons' fate, though, so they would never come to their aid.

Not after the war, when the angels and demons went their separate ways. I doubt there will ever be hope for true diplomacy. Not that I care. The angels are all pompous hypocritical assholes.

Except for the one beside me.

We haven't talked about what was said to us. Jezebel mentioned it as if it were common knowledge, but neither one of us suspected it—mates. The impossibility of it still dances in my mind, but the more I ponder that knowledge, the more it starts to make sense. From the beginning, Roux has stirred something inside me, something almost feral. I've wanted her since the moment I laid eyes on her, but I blamed it on my desire to make an archangel fall. It was a game, but a game I desperately wanted to win.

Now I know it wasn't a game at all, at least not between us.

Whatever trick fate is playing on us might very well get us killed. Demons and angels don't mate. They don't mingle for longer than brief interludes, and yet here I am, thinking of a way I can convince her to stay. I've considered caging her, but the thought of stripping her of her wings makes me sick. I've thought about never fixing the problem with the orb so that she'd be forced to stay in Soleil, but would she even choose to? I may be coming around the idea of Roux being my mate, but it doesn't seem like she is—though her jealousy is a welcome emotion.

The tunnels down to Soleil aren't hidden. The angels know precisely where they are, so I almost expect a battalion of the fuckers to be waiting for us to spring up. They can't go into Soleil after Roux without starting a war, but they would happily seize the opportunity to grab her should she try to run again. I'm surprised when they are not there, but I figure they decided that she wouldn't be foolish enough to come back to our realm for the moment.

Which means they are underestimating both of us.

"Shouldn't we have allowed the demon to show us where Abraxos's house is?" Roux asks, the dry, hot wind sweeping her hair around her face in a beautiful display. It makes me want to commission a painting of her just like this, with her eyes on me, a battle in her expression, and her wings spread out proudly as her hair blows around her face. The only thing that would make it better is if her lips were plump from me ravishing her.

"I don't need his help to find him," I answer, tipping my nose up to the wind.

Roux rolls her eyes. "So, what? You just snap your fingers and you know where he is?"

I meet her gaze, and the corners of my lips tip up. "Little unicorn, you're forgetting I'm the crown prince," I rasp as hellfire climbs along my shoulders and dances upon my head.

Her eyes flick up to the crown of fire and lingers, enamored. My hellfire reaches toward her and licks along her skin. She doesn't seem to notice, but I do. It all makes sense now. Every last bit of it makes sense.

"Come, he's this way," I say when I feel a tugging sensation.

During the day, there aren't many demons who visit the surface. Too many angels fly overhead, and many of the angels would take time out of their day to ruin a demon's afternoon, so they prefer to come out at night. There aren't many demons willing to risk that by living here, so it's easy to feel the tugging of hellfire in a single direction.

"Is Jezebel ever wrong?" Roux asks suddenly as I follow the pull.

Her words stop my heart in my chest. It takes everything in me not to look at her and spook the conversation away. The question feels as if it has more weight behind it than anyone else would realize.

It sits heavy on my mind.

"In all the years that I've known her, she's never been wrong," I choke out, my voice tight, and then, because I'm losing my mind, I give her the opportunity to escape the conversation. "If she says we need to find Abraxos, then that is what we must do."

Roux is silent for a moment, as if thinking over my words. I dare not even spare her a look. If I see panic on her face, it will crush me, and if I see hope... well, we wouldn't make it to the fallen angel. I would claim her here and now. "But has she ever been wrong about something like..."

I pause and risk glancing at her. "You're asking if she's wrong about us being mates."

Her eyes shutter, as if she's trying to hide her emotions. Archangels are masters of the act, trained to be stoic and strong and obedient, but I've learned Roux is anything but an obedient archangel. Still, I don't let it hurt my feelings. It's not like I was expecting this situation either, and it's certainly not an easy situation to be in.

"Is there someone in Celestia, an angel, who awaits your return?" I ask, looking down at the cracks in the earth. I haven't really asked, not point blank, and had wrongly assumed she might have a heart to give. It's not unheard of for mates to decline each other, though I don't have much experience with angel and demon pairs. If Roux has someone she's already given her heart to, it would be selfish of me to take her anyway. I'm a demon, and although I wouldn't care about some other angel's feelings, if it hurt Roux... I would give her what she wanted, whether that meant letting her go or giving her the wings on my back.

"There are no angels waiting for me except the ones who'd like to persecute me for a crime I didn't commit," she replies, tipping her head back to look at the sky. "But I do miss the skies of Celestia."

I understand that. Here, in the wastelands, even the sky is a bit shrouded by the clouds and smoke that always hang heavily in the air. I don't get the opportunity to fly up into Celestia often, but when I do, the air is so much cleaner and clearer, so I understand her longing.

"Would it be so bad?" I ask softly, slowly walking in the direction of the tugging again. She follows without question, trusting me.

"Would what be so bad?" she asks. I can feel her gaze on me as she tries to determine my thoughts. I've lived so long, she won't find it an easy feat.

"If we were mates."

I don't dare look at her. I'm the crown prince. I've been alive for centuries, have gone to war with her kind, and have killed for sport and necessity, but I'm afraid to see that look in her eyes. I want her to choose me. It was a game before, but now there's much more at stake, and I can't determine what might transpire and what might die.

After long seconds of silence, I finally glance over at her to find her already looking at me. The orange at the tips of her hair and along her wings somehow still sparkles, even in the wasteland, as if nothing can dull her shine. There are so many emotions flashing in her eyes, I can't tell them apart, and she's tense, as if her body is violently fighting against her mind.

I stand before her, my black wings relaxed in a way that I'm not, my hair swirling around my jawline. Hellfire flickers on my skin, lighting the way as it drags me both toward Abraxos and her. I wonder what it would do to her should we ever touch skin to skin. I wonder if she'll burn as brightly as she shines.

She glances away and blinks in surprise, the question momentarily forgotten. "There's a house."

My chest squeezes painfully. She doesn't have to answer. I already know what an archangel would think of having a Soleil prince as a mate. There's a reason there aren't such pairings. Demons and angels don't mix. I'm a fool for thinking things could be different and that she could want to be with me. She's been transparent from the beginning—she's only using me to clear her name.

With that thought in mind, I straighten my spine and throw my shoulders back. "Let's get this over with."

"Vetris," she murmurs, but I'm already walking toward the house, my hellfire dancing higher on my shoulders. Pain echoes in my chest, a reminder of what an idiot I am. I can hear her following me, her toes dancing over the cracked ground to catch up, but I don't turn toward her.

Let her chase me for once.

"Vetris, wait," she says, and then her thin fingers grip my elbow despite the hellfire burning there. It should burn her, but her hand latches on and doesn't let go. My flesh tingles with the feeling of her fingers on me and the hellfire kissing her skin. "Would you look at me, please?"

"So you can drive the nail in deeper?" I ask, staring at the house before us. It's crude on the outside, but I recognize it for the illusion it is. It appears abandoned, a prewar relic, but I can feel the presence inside. "No, thanks."

"How do you know my answer?" she retorts, pulling on my arm in an attempt to get me to look at her. "How can you assume what I would have said without allowing me to say it?"

"Because it's obvious," I growl, still refusing to look at her. "You've done nothing but try to get back to Celestia. I should have taken the hint."

"You said Jezebel is never wrong," she argues.

I've had enough. The pain in my chest makes me more brutal than I'd like to be. I turn toward her, taking in her eyes, the beauty of her face, and the sparkle of her wings as they arch over her back. "Then this time she is," I snarl as I jerk my arm from her grip.

Hurt flashes across her features so quickly, I almost miss it. I immediately soften, realizing that I'm being a dick, but the damage has been done. She takes a step back, putting more distance between us. If I thought that would scare Roux, though, then I'm sorely mistaken. Instead of getting angry and shutting down, she meets my eyes and tilts her chin up in challenge.

"I was going to say no," she declares, her expression fierce.

With all the emotions whirling inside me, I forgot the exact question, the wording I used. "No to what?" I hiss.

"No, it wouldn't be so bad having you as a mate," she replies confidently, her eyes hard. "But you're an asshole. I want you to know that too."

I open my mouth then close it when nothing comes out right away. Those were not the words I was expecting, certainly not from this archangel's lips. She wants to go home despite the way they have treated her, and I've been helping her get home, but she's saying she might be okay with me.

"You're not... rejecting it?" I rasp, staring at her in surprise.

"Perhaps we should speak about it another time?" she reasons, glancing at the house. "I think I saw movement."

"You would be okay with me as a mate despite what I am?" I ask in confusion. "Why?"

She huffs and puts her hands on her hips. "I suppose for the same reason you're okay with me being an angel," she growls. "There's really someone moving around in there—"

"Who says I'm okay with you being an angel?" I tease, my wings lifting a little higher.

A sound comes from behind me.

"Vetris," she says, her eyes on whoever is behind me.

I turn, taking in the large, older demon standing in the doorway of the shitty house, and arch my eyebrow. He has an enchanted weapon aimed at me despite the hellfire dancing on top of my head.

Irritation floats through me at him interrupting our conversation.

"You have exactly five seconds to get away from my door and take your business elsewhere," he threatens, his eyes hard.

"Do you know who I am?" I declare, standing taller.

"I don't care who you are, Your Majesty. Get fucked."

Roux snorts, trying to cover up her laughter, her wings shifting. Either way, I move a little more in front of her. That enchanted weapon looks like it might be meant for wings, and I'm not about to let the asshole tear a hole through hers.

"Abraxos?" Roux asks, stepping up beside me and canceling out my protective stance. I scowl over at her, but she's focused on the demon in front of us, her face hopeful.

"Who's asking?" the fallen demands. "I don't want anything you're selling."

"Not even if it's about the orb?" she replies, and he freezes.

Finally, he scowls and lowers the weapon. "You better get inside before the angels come to pick you off, archangel." His eyes take me in. "I guess you can bring your demon inside too."

Roux looks over at me and grins, waggling her eyebrows at me. "My demon, huh? Seems like I outrank you here."

Despite the situation and the fact that a battalion of angels could appear at any moment, I laugh.

Leaning down as she walks by, I whisper, "You can outrank me anytime, unicorn, so long as you let me worship you on my knees."

I have the pleasure of seeing her face flush just before we step over the threshold of the fallen's den, and the magic that washes over us nearly chokes me. Roux gasps at the feeling as the air surrounds us.

Abraxos chuckles, the room brightens, and my hellfire dims.

CHAPTER 19
ROUX

Abraxos is not what I was expecting.

He grumbles the entire time he leads us inside and to a door on the right, not allowing us to get a good look at his house. It's much bigger than it appeared from the outside and warm. I follow him down the small steps and into a huge, open-plan kitchen and dining area.

"Sit, angel," he demands, pointing at a wooden table which looks like it has been hand carved. The black, faintly glowing wood has original knots and marks across it, with six huge, matching wing-backed chairs surrounding it. Plants hang behind it, dangling before large circular windows.

It's a mix of greens and blacks, and it's homey. Hovering orbs fill the space, emitting enough light so it doesn't feel dark. My hand trails across the wood, feeling the pulse of magic there. "Is this light wood?" I ask, peeking over my shoulder to see him glaring at Vetris who throws himself down at the head of the table like a king.

"It is." He nods, glancing at me.

"It's brilliant. Whoever carved this must be very talented."

"She was," he says in a matter-of-fact way, his tone clearly ending the discussion.

Taking the hint, I sit carefully, looking around the space.

A huge shelf made of the same wood sits upon the wall before me, with small wood figurines decorating it, carved with exquisite detail. I want to ask more, but I can tell by the guarded look in his eyes that he won't answer. In fact, he might even throw us out. We came for answers, though, and we can't leave without them, so despite my curiosity about this recluse who lives in the wasteland with a house big enough for a family or a small army, I sit back and wait.

I try very hard to not think about my and Vetris's conversation before we were interrupted. When he turned away, his face shutting down, panic had wound through me, causing me to be vulnerable and to admit how much I truly want him.

I don't know where we stand, and I hate that.

He doesn't offer us a drink, making it clear we are unwelcome and that he wants us to leave quickly.

When he leans against a worktop and crosses his arms, watching us, I begin, "So the orb—"

"What's with the demon?" he demands. "You, I understand, but him?" He jerks his head at Vetris, who yawns. I throw him a glare, which he just winks at before focusing on Abraxos once more.

"Let's just say neither of us had any choice."

"Explain if you want answers," Abraxos sneers.

I take a calming breath and cross my hands like I was taught, stiffening my spine.

"They accused me of taking the orb. They framed me," I admit, and it's something I'm still struggling with. How deep does the corruption go?

"Of course they did." He grins, not the least bit surprised.

"They were going to kill me. I managed to escape, and they sent Vetris after me."

He snorts, and again, he's not surprised, which means he knows something about angels working with demons.

"I managed to... convince Vetris to help me instead." I shrug. "And now here we are."

"Here you are." He grins. "Convince, eh?" He looks at Vetris. "Bet it didn't take much convincing."

"What do you mean?" I inquire.

"Just that demons crave chaos and sticking to the angel trying to pull his strings was probably a good reason to help you in the first place. That, and he probably planned to betray and use you anyway."

I glare at Vetris, who rolls his eyes.

"Lies, unicorn, I would stab you in the front, not the back." He seems genuinely offended, so I let it go.

"Anyway, I've answered your question. The orb—"

"Why do you want to go back?" Abraxos asks. "I'm assuming you want to take it back and clear your name? Be reinstated?" I nod, and he uncrosses his arms and sits on the middle chair, watching me. "Why? Why do you want to go back?"

"It's... It's my home," I start, but then I stay silent, unsure what else to say.

"That's it?" he presses.

"It's where I belong."

Liar, something in me hisses.

"Says them," he snaps. "Tell me, angel, have you ever truly felt like you belonged there? Do you want to go back just because it's safe, because it's what you know, and you are taught to think Celestia is everything? Or do you want to go back because you are afraid that without it, without them, you are finally becoming something you were always meant to be and they didn't like?"

Fear pounds in me as I stare into his knowing eyes that see too much. My mouth drops, and I am unable to answer, so like usual, when I am trapped into a corner, I fight back.

"Why did you go rogue? Why did you become a fallen angel?" I ask, deflecting.

"Touché," he mutters and sighs. He rubs his face as he looks around. "Many reasons, some I'm sure you are starting to understand the longer you are away from Celestia. The control, the rules, the lack of freedom or choice... We—you are nothing but cannon fodder, a foot soldier not meant to think or find true happiness. All the good is stolen and taken away, until nothing but duty remains. I craved more. I craved excitement. I craved love and a family. I was a fool," he replies bitterly.

"Did you get what you wanted?" I question softly, reconsidering the man before me.

"For a time," he replies, looking around with a loving, pained expression.

"This big house, the plants, the colors... It was all what she wanted, the one whose carvings you appreciate... She was my mate, my demon, before she was taken from me" —his eyes lock on me once more— "by the very people you wish to go back to."

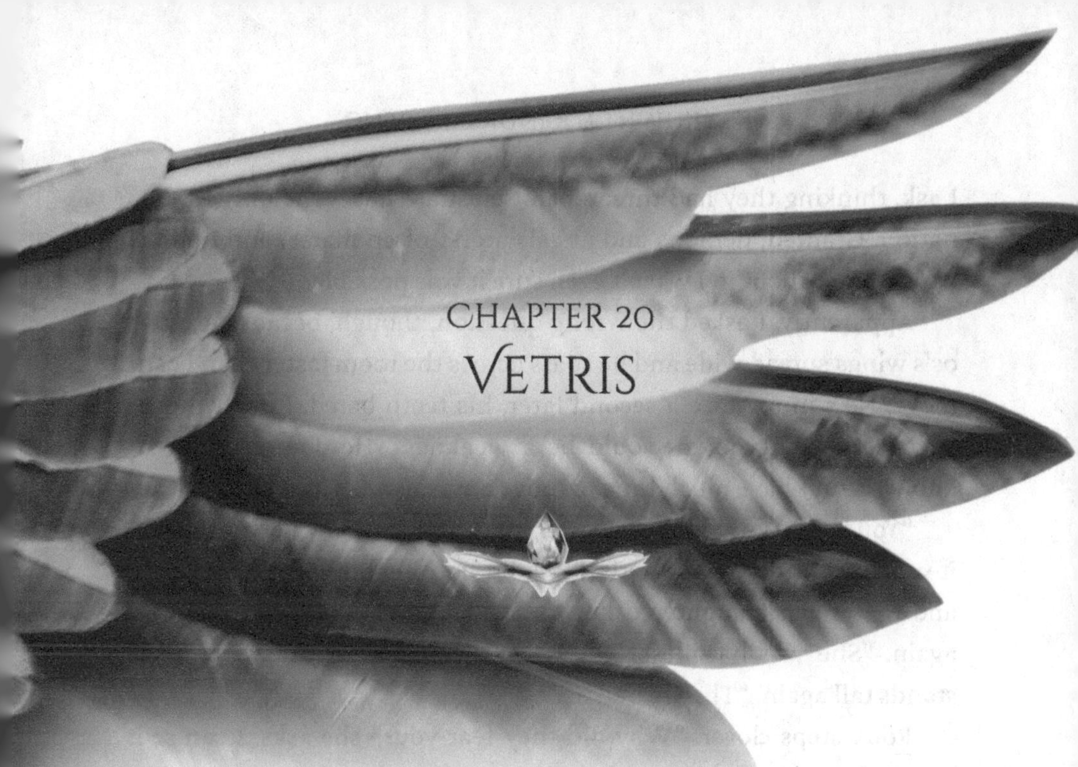

CHAPTER 20
VETRIS

I was bored as I listened to the two of them talk until those words left the fallen's mouth. I sit up, my eyes hard. "Demon?" I ask. "Did you say your mate was a demon?"

Abraxos looks over at me with a raised brow. "She was, before the angels took it upon themselves to kill her." His face twists with emotion, and an echo of his agony almost tears into me. I couldn't imagine anyone taking Roux from me. "They came in the night. We weren't hurting anyone. We built this house together, away from Soleil and Celestia, when it was still green and full of life." He hangs his head. "Before I knew what was happening, her head lay at my feet, and the seraphim were here to remind me of what I am." He meets my eyes. "She died because she loved me, and I have to live with that. I have to live without her. The other half of my soul is gone."

I blink at the pain in his eyes and the new information being given to us. Abraxos had a demon mate, but the angels killed her. I search my memory for some tidbit about something like this, but there's nothing. Abraxos is older than me.

"Why would they kill her if you weren't doing anything wrong?"

I ask, thinking they had threatened Celestia. That is the only explanation. Granted, demons and angels aren't often mates, and I don't know much about it. I wasn't even sure it was possible.

Apparently, I asked the wrong question, though, because Abraxos's wings spread wide and he soars across the room faster than I can move. He's in my face a second later, his teeth bared. I don't move because backing down would be a weakness. He doesn't have to know I didn't have much time to move anyway.

"You think we would do something when we knew how different it was to be mates?" he snarls. "We did nothing but love each other, and the angels slaughtered her for it." His face contorts with pain again. "She was harmless, a mischief demon." He leans back and stands tall again. "They feared us."

Roux steps closer. "Why did they fear you?" she asks. I can see her curiosity, and it's not lost on me that she sees a similarity between Abraxos and his demon mate and us. "What reason did they have?"

Abraxos finally gives me space, and I straighten and stand. I can't bear sitting down for this conversation, not when it suddenly has so much impact on my own life. I never considered that there was a reason demon and angel mated pairs were rare. I just assumed we weren't very compatible, but if that's not the case—

"Mated pairings are a blessing," Abraxos says as he reaches toward the shelf of carvings and picks up a tiny angel painstakingly carved to look like him. Beside it is a female demon. Both of them look happy, a difficult task to accomplish with wood. "But demons and angels don't mix, not because they shouldn't, but because the seraphim deem it so." He holds up the carvings. "When two angels are mated, they are just that, a mated pair. When two demons mate, it's much the same. But when an angel and a demon are fated, it's a far different story." He brings the two carvings together as if we're children in need of examples. "They feed on each other's power. The demon makes the angel stronger, and in return, the angel makes the demon just as strong. Together, they are powerful, more powerful than they ever could be apart, and the seraphim see that as a threat."

"That's impossible," I say just as Roux murmurs, "There's no way."

"Regardless of what you believe, that is the truth," Abraxos growls. "The two of you should know. You're walking in the same footsteps."

I freeze, going so still the only movement is from my hellfire. "What do you mean?" I ask hesitantly, my eyes going to Roux.

Abraxos snorts. "You think you can hide a connection like that, Prince? Just because you're in denial does not mean others can't feel it, and if I can feel it, so will the angels." He points at Roux. "They'll smell it on you the moment you return."

Fear suddenly clogs my throat. Roux's main plan has been to retrieve the orb and clear her name, but if what Abraxos says is true, she will be in danger if she returns. They'll kill her regardless of what she does. Not only have they ensured her death, but so have I.

"They took my wings as punishment and cast me out of Soleil. I'll never be able to return," Abraxos murmurs, tilting his head back as if he's in pain. "But I would also never want to return to a world that stole my love from me." He looks over at Roux with hatred in his eyes. "You wish to return to people who would murder you for who you love. Is that really what you want?"

Roux stares at him as both the fallen and I wait for her answer. "How do you know we're mates?" she asks.

Abraxos shakes his head. "Any higher angel can feel it, can smell the hellfire in your scent. They'll kill you for it. They kill everything. Our realm is slowly being killed by the angels, and yet you think you can trust them?" He shakes his head. "Be smarter than I was. You know what I say is true."

Roux and I share a look. There's been so much revealed here, and there's plenty to process, but from everything, one thing is undeniably true—Abraxos is not the bad guy. He's a fallen angel in mourning, a powerful one, but he's still just that. He's no threat to us, but there's still a bigger issue.

"Where's the orb?" Roux asks gently, focusing on Abraxos.

He clenches the carvings in his fists and holds them against his heart. "She would have loved you."

"Where is the orb?" Roux asks again, this time more forcefully. Her chin is tilted up, and she's a sight to see, one that I want alive.

Abraxos starts to laugh, as if this is all just one big joke. "It's gone." He chuckles.

I freeze. "What did you just say?"

His laughter spills out, and a crazed look fills his eyes. "It's gone. I destroyed it." He throws his head back. "Now the chaos they fear will reign."

Roux's face twists. "You destroyed it?"

"For her," Abraxos says, looking down at the carving of his mate. "Now everyone else can be free to love who they want."

Something squeezes in my chest, but whether it's approval or fear, I don't know.

"For her," he repeats, laughter still slipping out again. "I did it for her."

The carvings remain clenched in his fists...

CHAPTER 21
ROUX

"Have fun!" Abraxos calls as he tosses us out, his smile slightly insane as he continues to clutch the figurines. "At least this way, nothing stands in your way. You can be together. Don't be fools, not like we were. Don't fight it. Enjoy the time you have together, no matter how short." With that, the door slams shut, and Vetris and I share a long look.

Abraxos isn't such a bad guy. I can even understand why he did it.

Have I ever loved someone so much I would be willing to destroy the world for them? No, but the idea that I could doesn't terrify me like I thought it would. Instead, the notion that I could feel something so great and care about someone so deeply that I wouldn't be able to live without them excites me. It must be both addicting and consuming in the best way.

Is he right?

Is Jezebel? Could I have that with Vetris?

Not that it matters now.

My world crumbles around me, and the truth sinks into my

bones, making them ache, as the reality of what we are facing hits me.

Turning away, I start to walk as quickly as I can without running. I need space to escape my self-destructive thoughts, but it's no use.

You can't outrun what is inside of you. You can only live with it.

"So, what now?" Vetris asks as he keeps up with me.

"I don't know. I don't know! Okay?" I shout as I whirl on him, my markings lit up. Everything I was working toward, all my hopes and dreams, are crushed. There is no way home for me...

But is it truly home?

Is what Abraxos and Vetris said true?

Am I more than they told me, more than they tried to mold me into? Am I simply going back there because it's easier?

Either way, it is unnecessary now. I am never getting back into Celestia, and worse than that, our world, Celestia and Soleil combined, is in danger. I finally understand the feeling under me now. The world is unbalanced, and soon, everyone else will feel it, and both sides will turn on each other like they always do, pointing fingers. Wars will reign, and the death toll will be unimaginable. It feels inevitable, and here I am, staring at a demon, at a prince, who will lead his side while I stand with him.

I find myself searching his gaze for comfort, for anything, to tell me I'm wrong.

To tell me we are not doomed.

"Roux." He sighs and takes my hands, tugging me closer. I try to pull away, even as the comforting fire crawls along my skin, warming my cold, shocked heart. But why am I resisting? I no longer have a soul to save.

I've fallen, so why not fall a little more?

I let him pull me into his arms, where he rests his head on top of mine as he holds me tight, comforting me. We are two enemies, two people, who were never supposed to meet.

Two... mates.

"You won't face whatever will happen alone. They will have to come for you themselves, unicorn, and we both know how that will end." Pulling back slightly, he cups my cheeks. "They used you as a scapegoat. I don't know why, but life is unfair. It brought you to me, though, and I'm thankful for that, Roux, even if you aren't. They are playing a dangerous game, messing with mates and power and trying to keep us all in line to stop their hierarchy from being disturbed. If an angel mated to a demon is more powerful, then it would ruin everything for them."

"But what do we do?" I murmur, searching his gaze. "What do I do? I have nowhere to go. I have no home."

"You have me," he replies with pure, raw honesty. "We will figure it out, but first, let's get back to Soleil and somewhere safe." Stepping back, he holds out his hand, letting me choose. "Are you with me, unicorn?"

I see worry in his eyes. He believes I will turn away and choose the people who never chose nor wanted me over the demon fighting his own people to keep me safe.

How could I choose differently?

I lay my hand in his, feeling our powers surge together, and I know I'm not only giving him my hand, but my life.

I am giving him my answer to his earlier question.

Mates? No, it wouldn't be so bad at all.

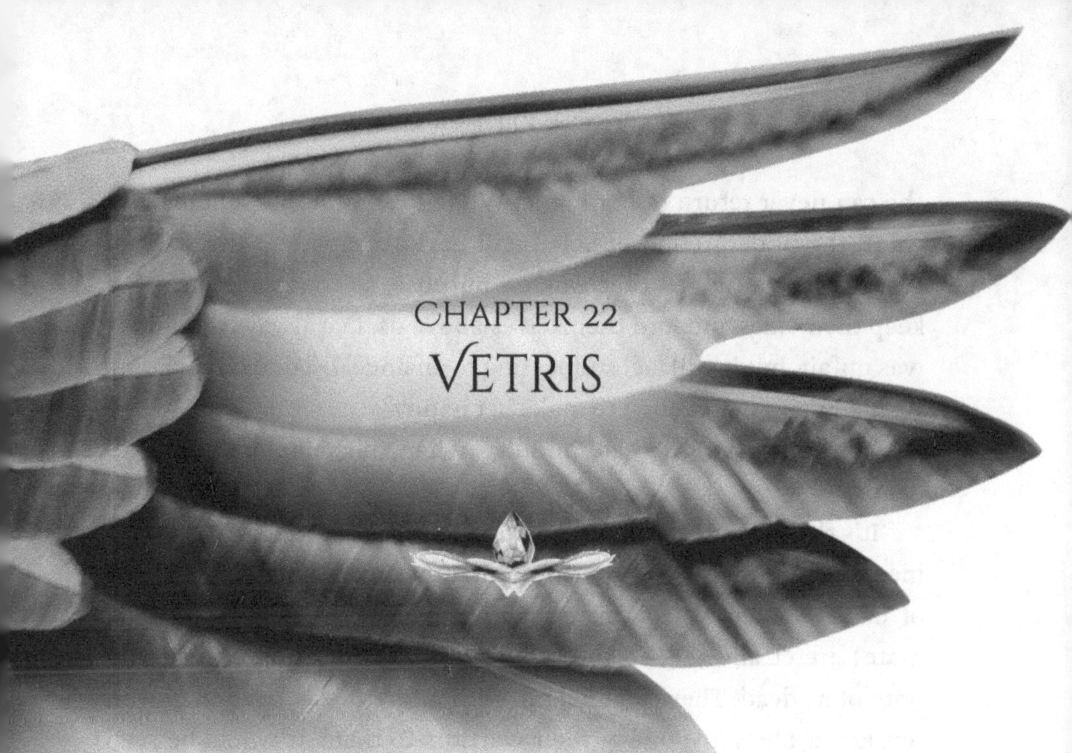

CHAPTER 22
VETRIS

I can't say that I know what to expect when it comes to this mating bond. I know it won't be easy, and that it will be considered a weakness, but if what Abraxos said is true, it could very well be a strength. Regardless, I'm a prince of Soleil, and the crown prince at that, and to think I'm going to march an archangel into my world and declare she's my mate? I don't know how I'm going to handle this. There will be those who disagree, but others will see it as something else altogether. Some of them will think she's a pet and nothing more.

I glance over at her. She's so much more.

I went into this as a bitter, bored demon who was annoyed that things seemed to have lost their appeal, and then she appeared, and the fire in her eyes tangled with the hellfire in me. I was lost, but in the best way. I've denied it, ignored it, and hell, I even tried to pretend it wasn't there, but the more I focus, the more I realize how strong the mating bond is in the first place.

Despite my clear acceptance of it, I still don't exactly know where Roux stands. She was just told all her plans are impossible, and that she can never return to her home. While I can offer her a home all I want, the underground of Soleil will never compare to the skies of Celestia. It's arranged that way on purpose, so that the angels can keep their skies and lord themselves above us. I've always thought it was unfair, but it will feel suffocating to an angel used to clear skies.

Can I give her enough to make her happy?

Would she ever be safe in Soleil when the seraphim want her dead?

It's then that I realize just how much is at stake here. The monumental chaos that will erupt the moment it's discovered that the two of us are mates will be historical. Abraxos said demon and angel mates aren't allowed, so the seraphim will attack harder, wanting both of us dead. They can't kill me without a true declaration of war, but Roux? She's just one of their warriors to them. It would be seen as them meting out punishment, nothing more—not that I'll ever allow them to steal her fire by striking her down. As the crown prince, I can consider it a declaration of war if they try to kill my mate, but... again, chaos.

Now, we must also deal with the aftermath of whatever destroying the orb means. I can already feel the instability in the ground beneath my feet, but it doesn't feel... dangerous. It almost feels like it's healing, and I don't know what to make of that.

Roux doesn't say much as I escort her down into Soleil. I can see the way she looks at everything in a new light, not as a different world but as the only world she can possibly live in now. There's sadness in her expression, and her wings droop a little bit. It's enough to make my chest squeeze painfully. I don't know how to make things better for her or if I even can. It's not like I'm used to uplifting a woman's feelings.

"Chin up, unicorn," I tell her, thinking maybe I can make her laugh. "At least now you can sit on my lap while I sit on the throne. You can tell me your wish list."

She scowls. "What, like a demonic Santa Claus?"

I grin. "You can either be naughty or nice." Leaning closer, I whisper, "I prefer naughty."

I don't even get a smile. All I see reflected in her eyes is pain, and I swallow my teases. I was heading in one direction, but at her look, I switch gears. "Come."

"Where are we going?" she asks, but she follows dutifully, trusting me. It means more to me than she realizes.

Eyes turn toward us as we make our way through Soleil, their gazes hungrily fixed on the angel at my side. They won't touch her while she's with me, but I'm going to have to do something to make sure they know whom she belongs to soon. Otherwise, she'll end up slaughtering every demon who dares to touch her. I don't doubt my angel for even a moment.

She'll leave a path of carnage, and the thought alone makes my cock hard and my heart sing.

When I drag her through the large double doors that lead to my throne room, she looks around with interest but also confusion. "You brought me to the throne room?" She glances toward the demons lounging on the side. "Do you have a meeting?"

"Everyone out!" I tell the demons. As one, they stand and saunter off, glancing at the archangel in curiosity, but they are not stupid enough to ask what's happening. They close the door behind them, and I flip a latch to make sure it stays that way.

Roux's eyes follow the action before meeting mine. "What are you doing?"

"You're worried, little angel," I murmur, stalking toward her. "I see the sadness reflected in your eyes."

She shrugs. "Of course I'm sad. I just found out I can't go home."

"May I offer a solution?" I ask. "Or rather an alternative?"

Tilting her head in question, she asks, "What's the alternative?"

My heart flutters with anxiety. It's the first time I've felt true fear in millennia. I walk over to the throne in the middle of the room. Hellfire dances along the walls, the symbol of power. It makes the space warm and comfortable and highlights the oranges in Roux's hair and wings in a way that makes me want to immortalize her in a painting.

Perhaps, after this, I'll commission one or a hundred.

Yes, I'll hang one on every wall of this castle.

"I could put another throne here," I murmur. "You could stay with me here in Soleil. We could be mates in every sense of the word."

She frowns. "It isn't like I have much of a choice any longer."

"You always have a choice," I reply, making sure she meets my eyes. My heart flutters in pain at her words. "If you say no, if you don't want to accept that we're mates, it'll fucking hurt, but I'll accept it. You'll still have my protection here in Soleil. I can arrange a house for you to stay in, and you'll have everything you might need."

It hurts to say those words out loud. It would kill me for her to be so close and yet so far, but I would do exactly that if she asked me to. The feelings I have for her, this need to protect and love her, is starting to choke me. It's so thick, I wonder how I can still speak.

I need her to choose me, I realize.

I need her to choose me even though it means having to go to war to keep each other. I need her to choose me not just because she has no other choice, but because she can't do otherwise.

I want her to... to want me rather than need me.

"You would do that for me?" she asks, her eyes alight with something I don't understand.

"I would do whatever you asked of me," I answer honestly. Before her, I am almost weak and powerless—a foreign concept for me, but true nonetheless.

Roux brings me to my knees without even trying to.

She takes a step toward me, her wings lifting a little. "Whatever I asked?"

I nod, my eyes greedily taking in the image of her lit by hellfire and burning it into my brain so long after my sight is gone and the world withers, I will remember her—beautiful, powerful, and mine. "You only have to ask."

She takes a few more steps and stops right in front of me. "So... we're mates?"

"We are."

Again, no hesitation.

I'm looking down at her, and I see desire in her eyes. Here, like this, I can see how beautiful she would look if she fell completely, if she let sin win, but I also like her as she is, this fierce warrior prepared to fight for anything she believes in. The desire to taste her hits me so hard, I clench my fists to stop myself from snatching her up into my arms and having my wicked way with her.

"Would you announce that to Soleil?" she asks. "Would you claim me publicly?"

"I can open that door right now and shout it if you'd like," I offer. "I'll post a sign on every board and declare it for all to hear. I do not fear the outcome, unicorn." My hands settle on her hips and pull her closer so I can lean in. The feel of her curves and her warmth under my palms makes me shiver and my voice hoarse. Never have I needed or wanted someone so badly. "I only fear losing you."

She startles in my hold, surprised at the profoundness of my words. Her lashes flutter, her eyes reflecting the hellfire surrounding us. For a moment, we say nothing more because the air is heavy with all the things we want to say. This won't be easy. If she chooses to stay, the seraphim will still want her dead. They'll send their warriors after her until she's known as a true enemy of Celestia, but she won't have to deal with that alone. I can protect her. I can stand by her side and fight with her.

But that can wait.

As she looks at me and I look at her, I realize there's only one thing I want to do right now. I don't want to argue or talk about the future. I don't want to think about the hell that's coming or the chaos our world will fall into soon. All I want is the angel before me, my unicorn, my mate.

I dip down, pausing with my lips over hers, giving her the choice. "Will you burn with me, little angel?" I breathe as my wings wrap around her. "Will you let the hellfire in?"

Say yes, I beg wordlessly.

Become mine, and let me show you what beauty there is in fire.

CHAPTER 23
ROUX

My eyes dart to his lips. He's so close I can almost taste sulfur, his skin burning against mine until I struggle to breathe. Yes, the fire. I blame the fire, not the desire clawing at my insides, desperate to come out. I want to drop to my knees and scream yes, and beg him to fuck me and make all my darkest and dirtiest desires come true.

I hesitate from fear, though, and he starts to pull away.

I know if I let him go now, I will lose him, and some part of me fears that more than I fear anything else.

More than I fear the war this will bring.

More than I fear losing myself in his fire.

More than I fear burning in hell.

Plastering myself against his chest to keep him from pulling away, I watch his eyes widen in hope and desire. I press my lips to the corner of his in a featherlight, teasing touch. "Yes," I whisper.

He's frozen as his hands clench my hips. "Say it again," he demands, his voice rough.

"Yes," I purr, rubbing my lips along his. "Yes, I want you. Yes, I need you. Yes, I'll be yours."

He shudders as I drag my hands up his arms, allowing myself to touch his hard, heated muscles. My pussy clenches at the strength, at the power, I find in his body, needing to feel it against my skin. "Well, Vetris, are you going to just stand there, or are you going to make good on all your promises?" I step back, and he automatically steps forward as if to prevent my escape. Smirking, I retreat farther. "Or was it all just talk, demon?" I taunt.

I laugh when he covers the distance in a flash and snatches me up. His hand goes to my ass, and he lifts me effortlessly. I wrap my legs around his waist with a groan as he nips my chin in punishment, his cocky smirk firmly back in place.

"Oh, little angel, you have no idea what I'm going to do to you," he purrs. "Let's start by shutting up that pretty mouth. The only thing you will be saying for the next week straight is my name." He nips my lip until he draws blood, and then he growls, "You'll be screaming it for all of our people to hear, until they know whom you belong to."

Gripping his hair in a fist, I yank his head back and watch as his eyes narrow. "If I belong to you, then you belong to me," I warn.

"Forever," he promises without shame or reservation. "So let's make it official, shall we, unicorn?" Turning, he strides over to his throne with me in his arms and drops me onto the huge gothic chair. Instantly, he kneels before me like he's prepared to worship my body.

He's beautiful, sin incarnate, and my heart and pussy clench in unison at the sight before me.

His hands slide up my thighs, parting them wider, and I lean back in his throne, making myself comfortable. "I've never knelt for anyone before, unicorn." I can tell by the vulnerable gleam in his eyes that he means it. "Only you. Now hold onto the arms, angel. You're going to need it." Just as quickly as the vulnerability came, it disappears into cocky commands, and I discover I love both.

"All talk," I taunt, lifting one leg and placing it on his shoulder. I raise my hips so I nearly press my pussy to his face. "Shall I take care of myself while you continue to talk?"

"I'd like to see you try. This pretty angel pussy is mine now, and if I have to tie your hands so you can never touch yourself again, I will."

"Still talking, are we?"

He lays a hand on my leg, and with a smirk, his hellfire crawls along my pants, burning them to a crisp until they turn to ash, leaving me bare.

"Don't you dare," I warn, but he leans up and does the same to my shirt, leaving me completely naked before him.

"That's better. This is how you will always sit on this throne, naked and wet for your mate." He smirks, his forked tongue dragging along my calf poised on his shoulder.

"What, and let your people see?" I try to tease him, but it comes out strangled, especially when his tongue slides higher. His velvety, bumpy tongue drags up my thigh, avoiding my pussy, and to the valley between my breasts, leaving me wanting and annoyed.

"Hmm, maybe you're right," he whispers against my skin. "Only I get to see you like this. I could blind them all so that I can see this view every day, but they can't."

"You're crazy," I murmur as his tongue darts out and curls around my nipple.

"Yes, unicorn, I am, and you just agreed to be mine." He grips my leg and wrenches it wider so I slide farther down the throne. "Now scream for me, angel."

"Make me," I retort.

This time there are no words, just a long, smoldering look that promises retribution, and I know I've pushed my demon too far. I can't help but grin, though, because I love how easy I can rile him up.

His forked tongue drags over one breast to the other, curling around my nipple and tugging until I moan. The flash of pain and pleasure shoots straight to my clit. I've always enjoyed the rougher side of sex, and the oblivion and pleasure that can be found in primal, painful fucking. The other angels couldn't quite get me there, but I know my demon mate can. He's going to obliterate any other traces of anyone else and claim every inch of me, starting with my breasts.

He licks and sucks on my nipples, pushing my breasts together as he leaves marks on my skin.

I gasp, my head falling back.

"Eyes on me, mate, at all fucking times. You will know exactly who is claiming you, touching you, and fucking you."

My eyes snap back to his, and my hips lift of their own accord, needing more. I need him to touch me, lick me, and fuck me. Smirking, he trails his finger coated in hellfire across my nipple, the heat intensifying as he circles it, and I moan and writhe.

"So sweet, so reactive. I'm going to make you come just by touching these incredible breasts, little angel, until you soak my throne and beg for my cock, and only then will you get it."

I whimper as he finally pulls his finger away, only for his mouth to seal over my nipple. He sucks one and then the other. My thighs are slick, and my pussy pulses, needing his touch. His fire crawls along my skin, heightening my pleasure. That's all that touches me, his mouth, and yet I'm on the verge of coming.

My hands scramble across the chair to find purchase, and my back arches until I thrust my chest more firmly into his mouth. I bite my tongue to stop a plea from escaping, but when his teeth dig into my breast, the sharp pain splitting me, it flows from my lips.

"Please, Vetris. God," I beg.

"Not your god, unicorn. Your devil," he purrs. "But I promise you the devil knows how to fuck better."

He attacks my breasts, showing me he was only teasing before. His fingers twist one while his tongue attacks the other. The pleasure grows steadily like the fires around the room as the crown prince crouches between my thighs.

His fingers brutalize one nipple as he bites the other, and I shatter for him, coming apart at the seams.

My hands grip the arms as I shatter for him and moan out my release, whimpering at the empty feeling inside me.

Sighing, he nips my breast once more. "That wasn't a scream, unicorn. Never mind, I'll try again."

He slides down my body. I watch him breathlessly, noting the red marks across my chest, and it makes something clench low in my abdomen. And then he's there, his demonic mouth pressing against my pussy. His fingers part me, and with a groan, his tongue darts out, tasting my need.

My surrender.

At the first touch of his mouth, every other thought disappears—the angels, the orb, the demons, the war.

None of it matters anymore.

Only this. Only us.

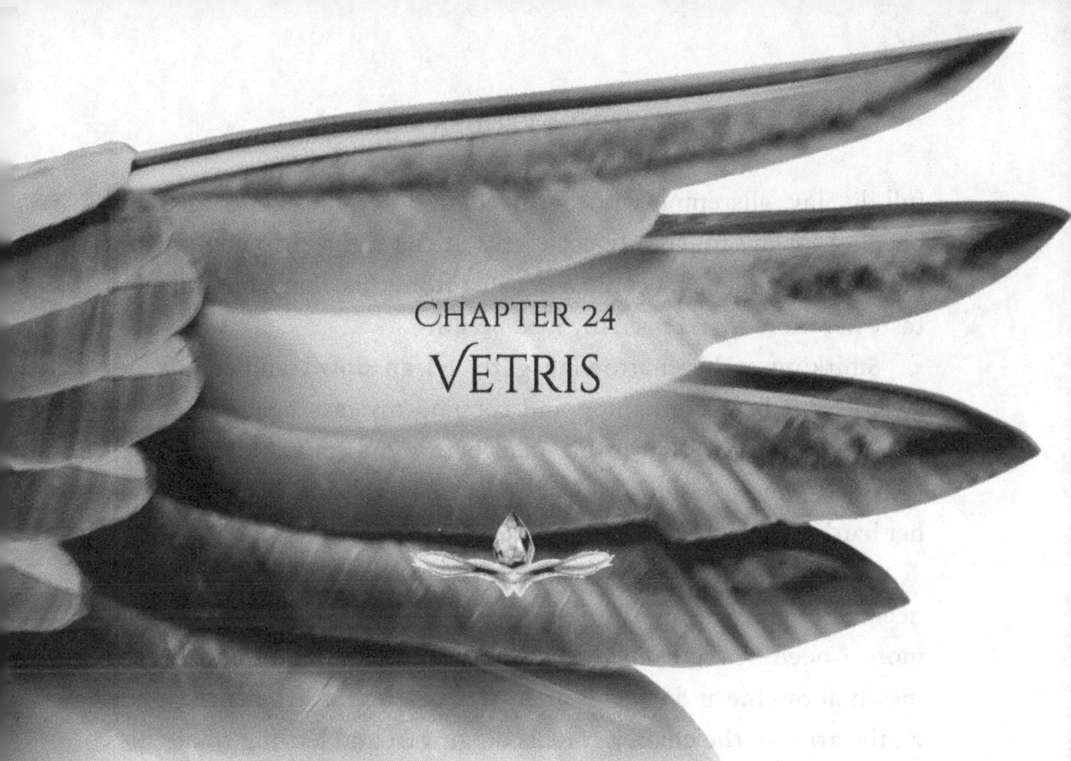

CHAPTER 24
VETRIS

I've imagined what fucking my angel would be like from the moment I saw her. I imagined throwing her against a wall, pinning her wings and throat, and fucking her until we're both raw with need and covered in sweat and juices. I've imagined destroying her in my hellfire and watching as she screams her pleasure while surrounded by my heat. I've imagined all of that, and it still doesn't compare to the sight of her spread on my throne, her face twisted with ecstasy as I kneel between her thighs. My cock is so hard it hurts, begging for relief. My length strains to get to my mate, to fill her, fuck her, and breed her. I'm so fucking desperate, and I know that when I sink into her tight heat, I'll be lost forever.

Fuck, she's so beautiful.

She's stunning like this, and when she's fighting or opening her mouth to give me sass. Fuck, do I love when she gives me sass. I'd like to use her mouth for other things and silence her bratty comebacks by sliding my dick so deep she'll gag for me, even as she begs for more.

Next time, I remind myself, focusing on my girl. My hands shake slightly when I press her thighs wider. Her pretty pink pussy is on full display, glistening with her need, and her clit is engorged and begging for my touch. My cock jerks at the sight, dripping precum along the floor. Fuck, I could come just from this alone, but I need to taste her more than I need my next breath

Smirking at her narrowing gaze, I lean down and inhale her sweet scent before groaning and rubbing my face against her wet pussy, coating my skin in her cum before my tongue darts out to taste her. The explosion of flavor makes me feral, and I snarl as I yank her harder against my mouth and feast.

My fires burn brighter for her because she makes me crazy, her need sliding down my throat until it's all I want to live on. I need more. I need her screams. As I swirl my tongue around her clit, she mewls above me and wiggles in my throne. Her fingers clench tightly on the arms of the chair, her nails digging in and leaving small lines in the wood. It gives me great pleasure to see she's leaving behind those marks, because there will be evidence of this moment there. When I'm dealing with business and seeing my people, I'll be able to run my fingers over those grooves and think about how she looks right now, with her legs draped open for me and her wings hanging over the edges of the throne.

She fights against throwing her head back and closing her eyes against my order to look at me while I drive her crazy with my tongue. I've had plenty of practice at bringing women to their knees, but I've never kneeled for an angel or anyone else. Not like this.

Only for her, my angel.

She is the only one I will ever kneel for. All others who came before her were forgotten when I first laid eyes on her, and my body is more hers than it has ever been mine.

I lap at her, circling my tongue around her clit and sucking, until she's writhing with need. I need to show my angel how good I'll be for her, and how I'll always make her come.

"Is this what you want, unicorn?" I ask, turning my head and nipping her inner thigh, my cock spilling more precum at the sight of my marks on her. She jerks against me, her eyes widening in surprise. "A demon worshiping you like a deity?"

"Yes," she hisses, grinding against my chin in an attempt to get me to return to what she wants. "Now fuck me."

"Patience, angel." I hum, stroking a finger along her seam. In retaliation, she lunges forward and wraps her hand around my wing where it meets my shoulders. Euphoria fills me at her touch. It's the most sensitive part of me, and when she strokes her fingers along it, I shiver, nearly coming from that alone.

"I've had enough patience," she growls before threading her other hand into my hair and pushing my head back down to her core. Anyone else would be dead for demanding my obedience, but not her. I find I crave it. She presses against me tightly, forcing me to lick her, blocking my ability to come up for air.

If I die this way, then so be it. What a way to go.

Fuck, the thought alone makes me come with a growl, and I spill across floor, but my cock remains hard, ready to mount my mate after I get what I want—her cum on my tongue.

She grinds against my mouth as I lick and suck her, her cries growing breathy and urgent. The scent of her need fills the air as she grows even more slick with desire. Her pretty pussy flutters, and I want to roar in victory. There's a pool beneath her I can feel with my fingers as I inch toward her core, tempted to stroke inside her with my digits and drag more urgent moans from her lips, but just before I can act on that urge, she shoves me backward. I'm surprised by the action and barely catch myself before I splay across the floor, looking up at her in surprise.

"My turn," she snarls, standing on shaky legs. "Sit on the throne."

White-hot desire fills me at the command. I ache to taste her cum, but how can I resist my mate? I would do anything for her. My cock is already hard, but it strains harder at the forceful way she looks down at me.

"You'd command a crown prince?" I purr. I don't bother to wipe my face, leaving her juices glistening there for her to see, my hands clenching with the need to drag her back to my face until she rides it and comes for me.

"I'd command my mate," she corrects, and that word hangs heavily in the air for a moment, neither one of us able to get past it.

Mate. Mates.

Fuck, she's my mate.

I move without consciously deciding to, dragging myself from the ground and striding toward the throne. Her hand stops me just before I sit down, and then she reaches for the clasp on my pants. She doesn't have her own fire to command like I do, but she doesn't need it. With pure strength, she rips the material apart, leaving me in shredded cloth. My cock was already free, but now I'm naked for her, and her eyes greedily soak up my skin. Pride and satisfaction make me puff up when I see the desire she feels for me in her eyes.

"I liked those pants," I say, grinning at her.

Her eyes flash. "I liked mine."

Fuck, I love this woman.

She shoves me onto the throne, my ass sitting in her juices. I have no time to adjust before she kneels before me and grabs my cock in her small hands. The sight of her like this, naked with her wings arched over her back, makes my cock jump. Holy shit, I'm not going to last long if she keeps looking at me like that. Aside from gripping me so sweetly, she hasn't really even touched me, and yet my hips shift slightly to fight the pressure.

"You said you've never fucked an angel," she comments, but it's more of a question than anything else. A knowing smirk graces her beautiful face.

"I haven't," I respond hoarsely, barely able to speak over my need.

A mischievous smile pulls at her lips. It should worry me, being at her mercy like this, but she could kill me right now and I'd die happy. I'd go with a smile on my face. She leans down and opens her mouth, and I hold my breath. Her warm breath dances over my tip, making my cock jerk again, desperately wanting to be encased in that wet heat, but she turns her head and instead presses it against her cheek.

"Tease," I hiss, grabbing the throne's arms and leaving my marks alongside hers.

With a husky chuckle, she glances up at me with those blue eyes that reflect the hellfire around us. "Hold onto the arms," she commands before she turns and takes me deep inside her mouth.

My eyes roll back in my head.

I try everything to stay focused on her as she begins to move along my length, down and then back to the tip, swirling her tongue, before dropping down again. It bumps the back of her throat where she constricts it, making my toes curl. Her wings languidly flap behind her, as if she can't help the movement while she conquers me. She may be the one kneeling, but she's very much in control.

The urge to take that control back is strong.

I thread my hand into her hair, holding her still while I pump hard up into her mouth. Fuck, she feels so good. When her nails dig into my thigh in warning, I hardly heed it, until I feel her teeth scrape against my cock.

I pause before she withdraws and stands. She wipes the side of her mouth with her thumb and looks down at me. The remnants of my pants still hang on my legs, and my boots are still intact. I'm probably a strange sight, with my large black wings spread around the throne. She stands before me, and even though she's naked, she looks like she's prepared for battle. Her hair is tousled from my fingers, and the red marks I left behind on her breasts make me ache to leave more permanent ones.

"Do you want me?" she asks, tilting her head.

I sigh. "More than anything," I admit, watching her. "More than I yearn for the skies."

For a being with wings, that's the most euphoria you find, but here in this moment, she's better than any flight.

Words fail me at the emotions I feel. Mates are rare enough, let alone a mate like this. I could have killed her in the beginning, given her to the seraphim, and never known. Things had to be just right for this to happen.

As if sensing my loss of words, she moves forward and straddles my lap, her thighs on either side of mine. I can feel her heat, her cream dripping down on me. My hands go to her hips, holding her steady, even though her wings do the job just fine.

She reaches between us and grips my cock, but before she sinks down, she looks into my eyes, and I see all the emotions there.

"I feel it too," she whispers.

I don't have time to think about the profoundness of this moment, because she sinks down on me, inch by hard inch. I only know the wet heat of her ecstasy as she drops down until she's fully seated on me. She's so fucking tight, wet, and warm my eyes cross. My fingers clench her hips hard enough to leave marks behind as I hold her still at my base for a moment, my cock jumping roughly inside her. I try not to come inside of her, waiting until she's ridden me and I've seen those incredible breasts bounce from the force of my thrusts. She moans, her pussy clenching around me.

"Fuck," I hiss through my teeth, my head falling back.

She braces one hand on my shoulder, her fingers tracing the muscle there, while her other hand reaches toward my wing and strokes it, and I nearly burst.

"You're so beautiful like this," she whispers, leaning in to glide her lips along my jawline. "At my mercy." Her fingers twirl through the hellfire along my shoulders, which is burning brightly because of her. It reaches out and strokes her skin, loving her just as I do. She nips along my jaw, leaving tiny bites of pain as she clenches her pussy around me, dragging a groan from my lips. Her lips move up to my ear. "I'm going to sit in the fire with you, Vetris."

And then she begins to move.

Her hips rock forward and back on my lap as she fucks me. I let her take control for a brief moment as her fingers stroke my feathers and make me a puddle of need. My hellfire travels along my shoulders and climbs her arm, licking at her skin until she's throwing her head back and whimpering in need. It's all I want to see, but I have other plans.

This is all too gentle, and I promised to make her scream.

With a snarl, I jerk up and grip her hair with one hand, wrenching her head back until her spine bends painfully. She cries out in surprise as the movement shoves her down harder on my lap. My other hand grabs the soft tissue where her wing meets her back, and together, I use those two holds to pound into her hard enough to bruise. I attack her throat and her collarbone with my teeth, biting viciously, leaving more purposeful marks. Her fingers grab at my shoulders to hold on as more fire climbs her skin and dances along her nipples.

I feel the first waves of an orgasm hit her, but I don't stop. Fuck, I'm not going to stop.

My girl likes my pain, likes it rough, and that's exactly what she's going to get. The angels had no idea what they had in their midst and could never satisfy a being like her, but I will, every day, for the rest of our lives.

Smirking internally at what I am about to do, I use my power to form a tail. Normally, I use this in battle but right now I use it to bring pleasure to my little angel. My tail slips from between my legs and strokes her backside, dragging along her ass as it pets that little hole. Her eyes pop open in surprise, even as her cries grow louder, but it's not a scream. Not yet.

I lean down and savagely bite her breast, drawing a bead of blood and licking it clean. The taste of her blooms in my mouth, mixing with the lingering taste of her juices, leaving me little more than a rabid animal. I jerk her down harder against my thrusts, no doubt making her back ache, but I'll carry her after this, because she will be spent.

"Scream for me," I snarl against her skin. I pound inside of her roughly, my fingers clenched tightly in her hair as her wings flap uselessly behind her. If she wanted, she could lift us into the air. I almost hope she does, even though I won't stop fucking her. "Scream."

My tail presses against her ass, and her cries grow shrill. My hellfire travels down her chest to her abdomen before spreading along her pussy, meeting where my cock slams in and out of her, lighting her on fire. She shatters again, the waves of the last orgasm rolling into a new one, making her shrill cries into the screams I seek as I continue to fuck her. My tail slips inside, and the screams echo around the throne room, sweet music to my ears.

"That's my angel," I growl, my voice thick with my own ecstasy. "Now come again. Come for your mate. Let them all hear whom you belong to, and who is fucking this pretty angel pussy."

As I pound my cock inside her, my tail moves in time with my thrusts, fucking her down onto me with relentless force. Her eyes roll back in her head as my fingers stroke along her wing, adding another layer of pleasure. I feel her tense around me, her screams growing hoarse, and then she yells my name, her wings flapping aggressively enough to lift us just the barest amount. I fuck her through it, my voice little more than snarls of pleasure. My stomach tenses as my release rushes to the forefront, and my cock jerks before I start to spill my seed inside her. Spurt after spurt has me groaning in ecstasy, and my body convulses beneath her as she writhes above me, her fingers digging into my shoulders and leaving tiny half-moons from her nails.

We collapse into the throne, her body turning languid as I release her hair and pull her closer, holding her limp body tightly. My tail relaxes, pulling from her, but I leave my cock nestled inside her, wanting to remain connected as long as possible. The only sounds in the room are from our heavy breathing and the hellfire roaring along the walls.

When I regain some of my sanity, I lean down and kiss the top of her head, holding her tightly as I absorb the power and my tail disappears. "I will be with you always," I whisper. My throat grows thick with all the things I want to say, but I can't get them out for fear of descending into a mess of declarations, so I swallow them down. There will be plenty of time for that later.

"Promise?" she asks weakly, sleep already trying to claim her. Her fingers dance along my chest before settling over my heart, her own reminder without words.

"Promise," I murmur. "The world will burn and turn to ash before I will ever give you up."

I don't know if she hears me, though, because her breathing evens out, and she slips into the deep, relaxed sleep that comes after a good fucking. I hold her tightly and bask in the moment, and eventually, when my legs grow strong again, I carry her to my bed and tuck her in. I slide in behind her and follow her into the land of sleep.

For once, I'm comfortable, nestled against her back.

For once, Soleil feels like home.

CHAPTER 25
ROUX

I wake up warmer than I have ever been. I am so comfy, and my pussy and tits ache in a way that lets you know you've been well fucked. My body is languid and almost unresponsive. Never have I given into weakness like that, but then again, never have I been fucked by a demon prince and my mate.

His arms tighten around me like he senses my thoughts. Turning slowly, I trace his relaxed, sleeping face with my eyes. He's almost vulnerable like this, and the insane urge to protect him fills me. He can protect himself, but as he sleeps, his heart racing in time with mine, I know I would kill and die for him. Something snaps into place in my heart, something that started the very first time I saw him. I've always heard mates talking about the obsession and need to be with each other at every hour of the day. Even now, my pussy clenches, desperate to have him inside of me again, and I want to see his eyes open.

Like I called to him, he groans, the sound husky and going straight to my clit, before his eyes blink open. "Morning, mate," he murmurs sleepily, pulling me closer. I expected for him to pull away, but it seems we have both given up fighting this, so I snuggle closer and rest my head on his chest to listen to his heartbeat, letting it steady me when the rest of my world is imploding around me.

"Morning," I reply shyly.

His hands stroke down my back and up again before one grips my ass and hauls me across him. He sighs happily. "I can't wait to wake up to you every morning," he mumbles into my hair.

My heart clenches, and I lift my head, scanning for… I don't know. Tricks? But all I see is honesty and vulnerability. "Me too," I reply, and it's the truth. For so long, I've been alone, just working, training, and sleeping, and I find myself pressing closer, absorbing his warmth and strength, knowing I'll never have to be alone ever again.

"Tell me about your life, unicorn. I want to know everything."

I giggle, and he spanks me, making me gasp. My thighs grow slick with need.

"I mean it. Where do you sleep?"

"I, umm, in the training house—" My response ends in a groan as his fingers part my pussy.

"Carry on," he demands.

"With others. It's crowded, too many wings—" I moan as his long, deft fingers slide into me and his thumb rubs my clit. "Too many wings." I drop my head to his chest, panting.

"Hmm." He chuckles. "What about during the day? I imagine you soaring in the sky."

"When I'm not in trouble for crossing boundaries or doing my own thing," I respond breathlessly as he fucks me with his fingers.

"My naughty little angel," he purrs. "What about friends?"

"A few, none that were too close." I gasp at his touch, my hips jerking as I reach for my release. The wet sound of his fingers sliding into my cunt is obscene and sexy as hell.

"Lovers?" he growls.

"Some," I admit with shame, and he snarls, moving his fingers faster.

"Be a good angel and come on my fingers for me. Show your

mate whom this pussy belongs to now," he snaps as I ride them. "Tell me everything about your life. If you stop speaking, and I'll stop moving."

"There's this waterfall..." I spout random nonsense, not even sure what I'm saying because I'm so focused on the building warmth inside of me and the slide of his thick digits.

Gasping, I grip onto his shoulders as he leisurely fucks me with his fingers. All the while, he asks me questions about my life, trying to learn everything. I struggle through the answers, fighting with concentrating.

Finally, it's too much, and with a cry, I come on his fingers like he ordered. Humming in satisfaction, he slides them free and lifts them to my mouth. "Taste how prettily you came for your mate."

With my eyes on him, I suck his fingers clean, tasting my own tang. He snarls at the sight, grips my hair, and yanks my mouth to his, claiming it as our hands roam across each other's body, learning every inch. We're so lost in each other that we're not alerted to anything being amiss until the door slams open. He's up in an instant and poised before me, hellfire flying through the room. I try to move around him to help once I get my bearings, but he blocks me.

"Mine! No one will see what is mine," he snaps back at me, his eyes wild, so I hold up my hands, knowing he's on the verge of losing his restraint.

The demon who surged in gapes at us.

"You dare interrupt me with my mate? You dare look upon her?" he roars, prepared to rip him to shreds for the slight. The only thing that stops him is the hand I place on his chest, calming him, because I sense the importance of whatever message this man is going to deliver. The demon looks terrified of what information he has to bring, but more so of his prince.

"My prince, I apologize. I wouldn't have interrupted if it wasn't urgent," the servant explains, flattening himself in a bow. "Angels," he rasps. "The angels are attacking."

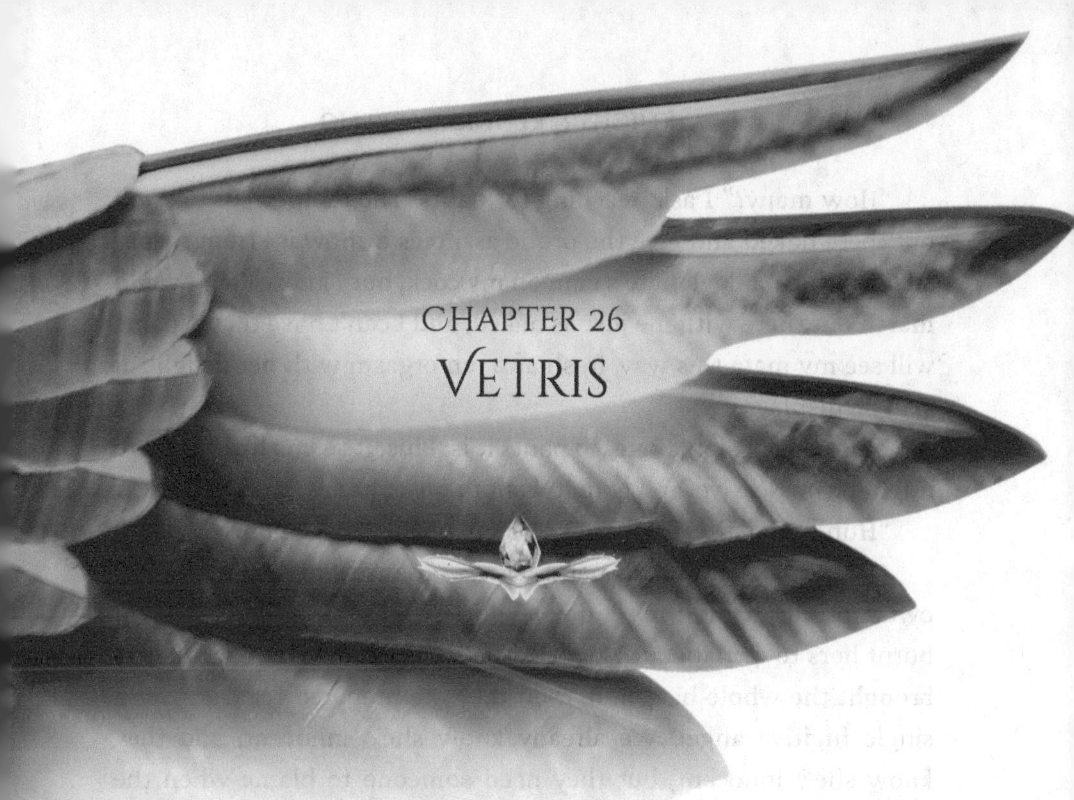

CHAPTER 26
VETRIS

The angels are attacking.

Those words take mere seconds to filter into my brain, bounce around, and come out with the realization that they have come for my mate. White-hot fury fills me at their audacity. They are attacking Soleil when they don't even know the true circumstances. All they know is that Roux is here. Likely, they are able to sense her, but plenty of lower demons could have been asked. They'd all speak of a beautiful angel strolling with the crown prince with just the smallest amount of pressure. They are not strong demons intent on proving a point, and they are not expected to be as powerful as the others, so I can't even be angry at them.

What I'm angry at is the angels for coming after my mate.

How dare they?

She is mine!

If they want a war, then they just got one. I will rip off all their pretty wings and hang them above my throne so no other will ever dare threaten my mate again. She's tense, and when she meets my eyes, I see both fear and determination gleaming in her bright gaze. She jerks her chin at me softly, telling me she is with me.

"How many?" I ask, reaching for pants. The temptation to stroll out there naked and give the prude assholes a show is strong, especially with my angel mate's cum on my cock, but I know Roux would march out there with me just as naked, and I can't have that. No one will see my mate this way, fresh after an orgasm with her delightful skin on display.

This is my vision alone, so pants it is. Plus, it seems like my mate might be possessive, and I don't want to upset her.

"Hundreds," the messenger croaks. "A whole battalion."

I freeze in fastening my pants, even as I sense Roux pulling on her own clothing behind me. I don't know what she's wearing since I burnt hers to a crisp, but I can think about that later. If Celestia has brought the whole battalion, then they are prepared for war over a single fugitive angel. We already know she's innocent, and they know she's innocent, but they need someone to blame when the world begins to fall into true chaos, and she's an easy choice.

But for them to bring so many after her...

"They are planning on a fight," Roux says, stepping around me. My warrior is calm and collected as she assesses the situation and prepares to fight.

I tense, thinking she may still be naked, but when I see her wearing one of my shirts, I relax. It's large on her, hitting her midthigh, and the neck is loose enough to slip over one shoulder and reveal some of my marks. I hum pleasantly at her, but there's still too much skin on display for her to be strolling before them.

"Procure some clothing for my mate," I command the messenger. "Immediately."

The demon bows and scurries off, his eyes wide with fear.

"This is bad," Roux murmurs, worrying her bottom lip between her teeth, only letting her concern show when the demon is gone. It pumps satisfaction through me when I realize she feels like she can be raw with me. "For them to send so many—"

"It doesn't matter," I growl. "They won't get you."

"But they are here to fight," she retorts, her eyes on mine. "They don't intend to leave empty-handed. The seraphim don't take too kindly to loss, and I expect when it's something as important as the orb, they won't stop until they have a scapegoat. I don't want—"

"Stop it," I growl, cupping her face between my hands so she meets my burning eyes and sees the truth. I would destroy this whole world to keep her, and I would burn every angel to a crisp and walk through their ashes. Her eyes widen at my tone. "No matter if they came here for a declaration of war or not, it doesn't matter. They will not have you."

"What if it *is* war?" she asks, her hands shaking as she reaches up and circles my wrists, using me as an anchor. "What if they came to destroy Soleil?" I laugh, and it only makes her eyes narrow on me. "I'm serious, Vetris. If they are here to destroy the below, I don't want that stain on my soul."

I can't help the genuine amusement that falls from my lips, but I manage to contain it enough to speak. I run my thumb along her cheekbones, taking in the sight of her fear for my world, a world I hope she remains in.

"Little angel," I murmur, tilting my head, "we have been to war for far less. We have spent millennia fighting with Celestia, arguing over petty squabbles, and hating each other. We are no strangers to their propaganda or their desires, but if they have come here to destroy Soleil, well, they can try. We are not so easily squashed."

"Demons will die," she whispers.

"And so will angels. It's an unfortunate fact of war, but I will not force my people to fight. They will choose to. This, Soleil, is our home, just as it's now yours if you so wish. There's nothing more noble than protecting your home."

She bites her lip, her face pinched with worry as she looks away. "You're sure I'm worth all this trouble?"

She thinks she's not and that this would be better solved by me handing her over to the seraphim. Growling, I jerk her gaze back to mine and bare my teeth.

"I've never been so sure of anything in my entire existence, unicorn. I will not be giving you to the seraphim now or in the future. You are my mate, and therefore, you are mine. I do not give up what is mine. Understood?" My words are rough and aggressive, but I'm angry that she would think I am capable of taking such an easy and devastating way out.

She blinks, and a glassy film covers her fiery irises. My heart twists in my chest at the sight of her rising tears. "No," I command roughly, and then my voice softens. "No, no, no. Don't cry, little angel. I didn't mean to be so harsh."

She laughs through the tears that suddenly begin spilling down her cheeks faster than I can catch them. "I don't mean to. It's just... You're perfect."

My ego inflates. "Well, obviously, yes. I've been telling you of my perfection since we met," I tease before pulling her into a hug. "We can handle this, Roux. There's no need to worry. Despite what you've been told, Soleil is not a realm of cowards. We will fight, and I will fight for you, until the very end."

Her arms squeeze me tightly as we embrace, her fingers digging into the muscle of my back. Everything I've ever dreamed of, that I never truly dared to dream of, is right here in my arms, and the seraphim have come to take that away.

The messenger demon returns, sliding back into the room, his arms full of various types of clothing. It's clear he hadn't been certain what kind of outfit my mate would like, but the fact that he came with every possible option endears him to me.

"Your name?" I snarl at him as he drops the clothing in a pile on a nearby table.

He falls all over himself, his hands wringing in front of him from nerves. "Gerkun, my prince."

"Gerkun." I nod. "When the war concludes, you will be my mate's servant." Roux startles, her brows furrowed, but I continue. "Have you alerted the other princes yet?"

"I'm honored, my prince. Only Nessanya has been alerted and has been seen heading toward the angels."

I curse. If Nessanya goes to face the angels alone, then she will start the war before we ever get there. As the descendant of Lilith, she's a savage demon, quicker to destroy things before she seeks any answers, and I don't need her to be killed by the seraphim. Nessanya often forgets she's not the crown princess, considering she was one prior to me. Never has a demon been more bitterly venomous than her.

I gently push Roux toward the pile of clothing, urging her to get dressed. "We need to hurry."

She immediately sifts through the fabric, finding a pair of leather pants that I just know are going to make her ass look like heaven and a strappy shirt. They are clearly the clothing of Soleil, and I wonder what the seraphim will think of it, but there are bigger things to worry about.

Turning to Gerkun, I point at him. "Alert the princes," I command, and he immediately begins bowing and backing from the room.

Before he can get too far, I call, "Oh, and Gerkun?"

He stops and meets my eyes. His are deep black pits with a speck of yellow in the center. "Yes, my prince?"

"While you're at it" —I grin— "wake the hellhounds."

CHAPTER 27
ROUX

I stop with the skintight leather pants pulled halfway up and arch a brow at my mate. "Hellhounds?"

He grins at me. "Tricky little beasts, but they sure as fuck love war and blood. They will protect you alongside me." He turns away, grumbling, "If only they fucking listened to me."

I can't help but giggle, imagining my very serious demon prince fighting against a horde of hellhounds to get them to stop destroying his stuff. He winks over his shoulder before heading to a doorway. Opening it, he steps inside and disappears. I take the time to jump and wiggle into the pants. Once they are seated low on my stomach, showing off my runes, I test their strength and movement, and find they are almost like a second skin and easy to move in. I yank on the top, and it settles against my skin with a hum, molding to it. I braid my hair back and smile when I grab a segment of Vetris's ripped pants to use as a tie. When I look down at myself dressed in all black, I can't help but laugh.

I look every inch the demon's mate, and I'm not mad about it.

I wait for Vetris, almost ready to go after him before he emerges again.

He steals my breath as he walks back in, his hands fixing the last piece of metal to his chest. The gold, black, and red breastplate covers his pecs and then moves along his wings in metal feathers that harden and protect them. It straps around his middle, and leather pants are slung low on his hips. His hair is styled back, and fire coats him as his crown appears once more.

He's fucking incredible and all mine.

Like he knows my thoughts, he grins at me. "Later, my horny angel."

"You are wearing that in bed while I ride you," I declare as I yank on some boots.

"Shit." He reaches down and rearranges his hard cock. "Don't tease, little angel, and make me hard. It's no fun going into battle with an erection."

Stopping before him, I grip his length through his pants, making him moan as his eyes slide shut. "I don't know. They might see this huge mound and run away." Laughing, I release him. "Now, mate, where are your weapons?" When he just stares at me, panting, I arch a brow. "If we are going to war, we will be prepared. So, my prince, where are your toys?"

Smirking, he heads to a wall and waves his hand. Flames rise and burn away the coverings hanging there, and an entire wall of weapons appears. From maces to cannons, there is literally anything a warrior could want just hanging in front of me.

Vetris plucks a huge sword from the middle. It burns with flames, exposing demon language on the blade that lights up with his hellfire and declares he's in charge. It's so large, he has to hold it with two hands, his muscles bulging in a way that makes me want to run my tongue along them. Fuck. It seems I'm doomed to march into battle wet between my thighs.

"Now you, unicorn." He watches me hungrily like this is foreplay. I have to admit there is something very hot about a man who knows how to handle a weapon. There's something even hotter about watching my mate grip that sword like he would hold his cock.

I'm just about to choose when the door slams open again. Both of us spin at the sound, prepared for the war to spill in, but when we see it's only Gerkun, we relax.

"My prince," Gerkun, my new servant apparently, shouts. "The other princes have joined the princess. Um, the angels look mad."

"Those fools will end the war before I get to join in," he mutters and kisses me swiftly. "Choose your weapons and meet me up top. Gerkun will show you the way. I'm going to talk with my family." Then he sweeps out of the room like the crown prince he is.

Turning back to the weapons, I pull out a sword and test its balance before sheathing it. I add some knives to my boots and my hips. There's a chain hanging on the wall with a sharp point on the end. I have an idea to add hellfire to it now that Vetris's hellfire can touch me so easily, so I coil that at my hip. Even if I can't use it, my mate certainly can. I also strap on a small crossbow I find before putting as many bolts in the holder as I can. When I glance back, nerves cover Gerkun's expression, but there's some other emotion too—excitement.

"Do you have a weapon?" I ask.

He shakes his head. "No, mistress."

Plucking a knife from the wall, I test it before throwing it toward him. He catches it with a yelp, but seems confident enough with it when he grabs it by the proper end. "Stay behind me, okay?" I demand when I reach his side. "I would hate to lose you before you can serve me," I tease and then storm from the room, heading toward my mate and the angels.

Gerkun scrambles after me, and I hear the hounds of hell bay in the distance.

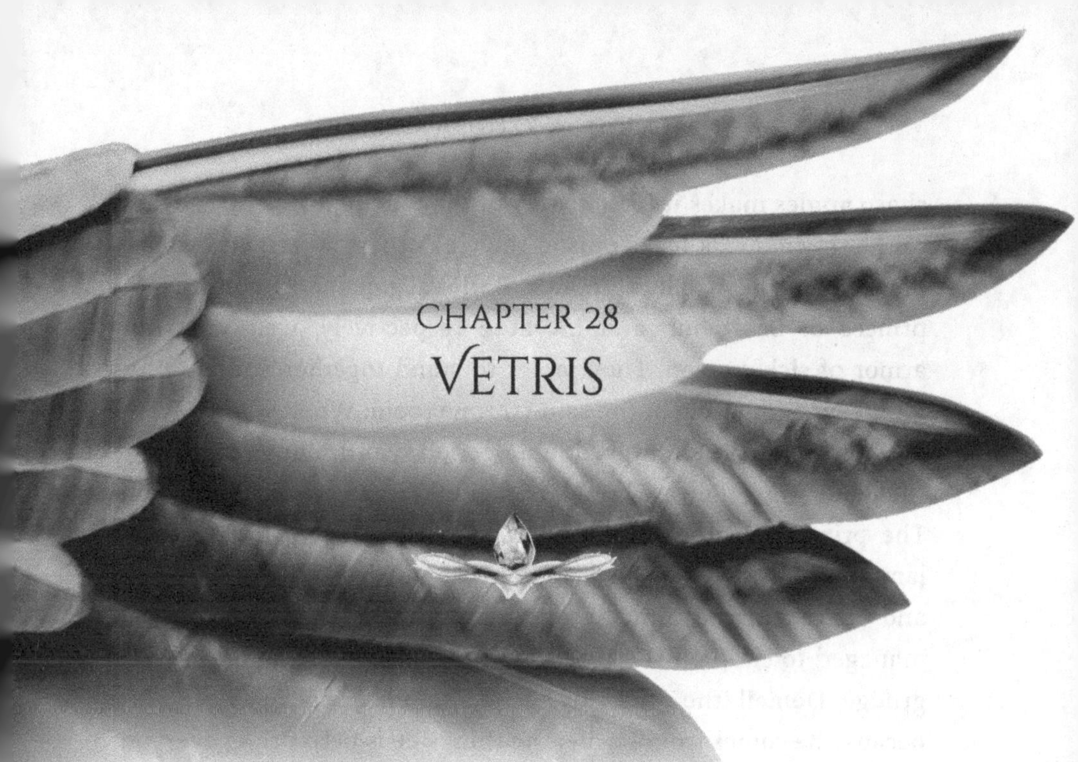

CHAPTER 28
VETRIS

Everything inside of me revolts at leaving my mate back in that room. Part of me is pleased that she's safe as she picks weapons, while another part of me hates that we're apart and she's not here to see the looks on the angels' faces as I step onto the street with my hellfire blazing and angel dust smeared into my skin. The seraphim's eyes immediately go to the glittering specks, his face twisting into a scowl. No doubt he thinks I am holding her hostage as some sort of sex slave. Leave it to the seraphim to assume demons don't respect consent. We certainly have a better track record than they do.

My family stands at the front, their own armor strapped onto their bodies. When I step up, it completes our eight. My six brother princes glance toward me, their appearances as different from each other as I am from Roux. Sablo, the prince of Belphegor, stands with his signature pickax thrown over his shoulder. His armor looks like melted metal was poured over him, but the asshole prefers drama. He's a fierce fighter and will be instrumental in whatever battle that will come our way. Ariuk, the prince of Mammon, is similarly wearing armor that tricks the eye. A series of sharp angles makes it look deadly to the touch, just as he is deadly to the touch. Ariuk leaks poison the way others sweat, an inconvenience when he also likes to fuck. Both Val'gan and Ar'gonneth, the princes of Beelzebub and Livyatan respectively, wear matching armor of sickly green. They prefer to stand together and are often found spending time in the same throne room. Wherever one is, the other one goes. Their large, double-edged swords hang languidly at their sides as if they are bored. I wouldn't be surprised if they were. The prince of Satan, Eramog, casually leans against the nearest lamppost, his eyes on Rael. He's never much liked the seraphim, and I can't blame him. At one point during the last war, Rael managed to chop off the tip of Eramog's wing. He's still holding a grudge. Domeil, the prince of Lucifer, stands as cocky as ever. Just because he comes from Lucifer, he thinks he is better than everyone else. His signature morningstar hangs at his side, waiting for an opportunity to be used. When I glance at him, his eyes are closed, as if he's sleeping. Knowing him, he probably is, but he'll be awake for any fight. He always is.

As I step out onto the street, Nessanya turns and scowls at me. "It took you long enough, pretty prince. I could have already ended this war and slaughtered them all before you deigned to appear."

I heft my battle sword over my shoulder and grin at her. "I was indisposed."

Her eyes trail down to the angel dust on my pecs and the marks still on my skin, taking it all in. She leans closer so that the angels can't hear her. "So then the rumors on the streets are true?"

I nod in answer, not confirming anything out loud. I doubt the angels know exactly what they have come here to fight for, and I'd like to keep that secret from them for as long as possible. I'm reminded again of Abraxos's story, of how he lost his mate due to the seraphim, and so it's the only answer I give.

I will not lose my unicorn.

"Where is she?" Nessanya asks, her expression eager. "I can't imagine the woman who would willingly spend her life with you."

"Just as I can't imagine the man who would do the same with you," I tease back. "And yet here we are."

I glance at the demon standing beside her, an incubus who only has eyes for one demon these days. He's dressed in armor that matches Nessanya's, and his eyes are fierce as he prepares to fight beside his own mate. Jaoel is a nice enough demon, and far kinder than most, which is why it's such a surprise that he chose Nessanya as his mate. Normally, you can find the incubus shirtless, wearing nothing but leather pants to display the tattoos etched on every inch of his skin. Today, he hides all that to go to war. The other princes remain unattached, but each of them is prepared to fight for Soleil. We all know this moment well and had fought in the last war with the angels. It almost feels good to be in this same position again.

As the crown prince, it's my duty to have talks with the angels to see if there's a way to settle this all peacefully. I know there isn't, and I know what they'll say, but it's still a duty I must uphold.

"You march into Soleil bearing weapons of war, your warriors are armed for battle, and you stand in our streets with ill intent," I declare. The soft murmuring of voices stops the moment I speak. My hellfire dances along my shoulders, and the fire crown on my head glows for all to see. Hellhounds begin to stalk along the edges of our gathering demons, feeding off of the tension between two armies. "State your business," I say, my chin high.

Rael stands in the front of the army, his large, perfectly white wings spread in a show of force and purity. Certainly, when I think of purity, it's not this asshole in front of me. Roux is far purer than this winged shit stain, but still, his propaganda is strong. Dressed in his own glittering golden armor, Rael has led an army here to slaughter an innocent archangel. The other seraphim behind him watch in with both curiosity and eagerness, as if they don't exactly know why they are here but are looking forward to a fight.

"We had a deal, prince," Rael answers, his eyes narrowed on the glittering dust along my chest. "I believe you have something that belongs to me."

Fury fills me at his assumption that Roux belongs to him. She belongs to no one but me! I push the fury down, however, because now isn't the time to attack in anger. A good leader is levelheaded and strong.

"There is nothing in Soleil that belongs to you," I respond, staring at him.

Rael tilts his head. The angel battalion lined up behind him shifts at his movement. Demons continue to join our ranks, those who are coming from far and wide across Soleil. No doubt, many of them are making sure their young and vulnerable are protected. The angels have a history of targeting them first, and we've learned over the years. Many homes in Soleil have panic rooms that can't be opened by anything other than a demon. If I were an arrogant demon, I'd have locked Roux in one for protection, but my angel would never forgive me.

She's a warrior through and through.

"The dust on your skin says otherwise," Rael comments, the tone in his voice dropping an octave. "You've had your fun with her. Now it's time you hold up your end of the bargain."

My family glances at me. If the rumors have been flying around Soleil, then they likely know just as Nessanya does that I have no intention of sending Roux with these assholes. They also likely know that I love drama when it comes to shit like this. I thrive on it.

I wink at my closest brother and grin at the seraphim. "The deal is off. Obviously."

His face visibly reddens in anger, but he holds it together. Seraphim have to uphold a reputation of serenity, and Celestia forbid he break it. "I'm a reasonable angel—"

"Not what I'd call reasonable," Nessanya interrupts.

The red on Rael's face brightens. "As I was saying, I'm a reasonable angel. It seems you've taken a liking to the fugitive, but playtime is over. Give her over to me, and I won't burn your city to the ground."

The demons around us hiss at the threat, their weapons rising higher. No one threatens Soleil, especially a prissy angel.

The hellhounds along the edges snap and growl at the angels. A few of them shift in discomfort, as if knowing what they are about to face. They are in our realm, so a fight will be in our favor. In the underground, wings are nothing but pretty ornaments, easily sliced clean off. There will be no battle in the skies unless we spill onto the surface. They will have to face us at our level.

"You really have some balls, don't you?" I goad, grinning at the seraphim. "So desperate to hide what you've done that you're willing to kill an innocent angel for your precious games."

The archangels glance at each other in confusion.

"I know nothing of what you speak," Rael declares, ever the snotty angel. He even sticks his nose up in the air. What a prick.

"You know nothing about the orb that was stolen, the orb that keeps Soleil and Celestia separated by death?" I ask, dropping bombshells. "You know nothing about the demons who stole it in the night for an angel you wronged?" I hardly pay attention to all the demons and angels who blink in surprise. "You know nothing about the slow death of our realm your kind have caused with such tactics?"

Rael doesn't react, not outwardly, but when his eyes meet mine, I can see the knowledge there. They knew exactly what they were doing, and the prissy angels assumed Celestia would be untouched in its place high in the sky, but Soleil would be hit first. It's what they want, what they have always wanted. They think they are so much better than us just because they are angels.

"You speak nonsense," Rael retorts, as if his word is law.

"Such nonsense that you would hire and make promises to the Crown Prince of Soleil to make sure a single angel is punished for your mistakes, hmm?" I goad. "After all, we had a deal, didn't we?"

Rael's face twists into a snarl, his anger getting the better of him. It gives me great pleasure to see his shell crack. "You're harboring a fugitive angel, demon, and therefore a declaration of war over a simple toy!"

I laugh at him, an open, full-bellied laugh. "You picked the wrong day to come down to our level, Rael." The demons around me shift as one, prepared for war. "Leave now and we might forgive this slight. As it is, we've been itching for war."

Rael doesn't back down. He waves his arm, and the battalion shouts some stupid hurrah and falls into a battle stance. My angel used to stand in their ranks, and now she'll have to fight against people she once knew, people she probably called friends to some extent. It saddens me that I'll have to slaughter them, but only for her benefit. I'm most definitely going to enjoy this.

"Where is she?" he snarls. "She must face her crimes!"

"The only crime she ever committed was trusting her seraphim to protect her." I wink at him. "That's okay though. She has a crown prince to protect her now."

Rael's wings snap out. "She belongs to Celestia!"

"You're cute when you're angry, you know that?" Nessanya teases, her husky laughter filling the street. Leave it to her to taunt the seraphim.

Her words only make Rael feral. So much for his reputation as a serene leader.

"Why you..."

He falls into silence, his eyes training on something behind me. I know who it is before I even turn around. I know what she looks like, but still, as I turn and take in the sight of Roux highlighted in the doorway, it takes everything in me to school my expression and give nothing away. Her wings are spread wide, the oranges at the edges glowing with hellfire. Her orange hair dances around her shoulders in the wind that same fire generates. Dressed in Soleil clothing and sporting a sword from my arsenal, she looks every inch like she belongs to me. Her runes flicker fiercely along her arms, highlighting the honed muscle there. My mate. My warrior.

Fuck, I love her.

Rael bares his teeth at her. "Fugitive angel. You're ordered to come with us or suffer the consequences."

Despite that command, that sweet little angel can't keep her eyes off her demon, her lips pulled up in a half smile that has me hardening in my leather pants. Fuck, what I wouldn't give to have this fiery angel bent over right now. It makes me want to kill the seraphim even more for interfering in this moment and making me wait to take my angel again.

A few of the hellhounds stalk over to her, their hellfire dancing along their spines. They take up stances at her sides, baring their teeth in savagery and bumping against her. She doesn't react, though I know she wants to. I'm sure it's confusing, but not as confusing as it is for me to watch her trail her fingers along the closest one's fur, petting it—and the beast fucking lets her!

I watch, enraptured, as Roux looks the seraphim in the eye, unflinching. She doesn't back down or cower. She doesn't act like an archangel at all. Instead, she points her sword at him in a threat, a promise.

Then, with every ounce of warrior in her blood, she tells him, "Fuck you."

If I wasn't already in love with her, I'd have ripped out my heart and gifted it to her right then, blood and all.

The seraphim loses his shit, bellowing about proper etiquette and some other bullshit I don't pay attention to.

All the while, she pets my hellhounds like they are ordinary earth dogs.

Fuck, I'd kill for this angel.

I turn and focus back on the angels before us, a feral smile pulling at my lips.

In fact, I plan to do just that...

CHAPTER 29
ROUX

Walking out into the middle of a standoff between angels and demons should terrify me, but it doesn't, not with my prince staring at me with eyes alight with obsession and love. Knowing he would rather fight a war than hand me over makes something inside me sing.

"I like her," a female demon near Vetris says. "She's going to bust your balls for eternity."

"I can't wait." Vetris smirks. "Now, where were we? Oh, right, I'm going to rip out your sinner heart and give it to my mate."

"Mate?" an angel calls, and a ripple goes through both crowds.

For a moment, all eyes turn to me. I sink my hand into the fur of the hellhound at my side, absorbing the warmth and comfort it offers before tilting my head back. Lines and lines of demons surround me in all shapes, sizes, and colors. Some are still dressed in their work outfits, and others are hissing, ready for the fight. More clamber from the walls and under the earth, amassing as they hear the alarms and join together.

The surrounding streets are silent, as if they have practiced this a million times, and there, in the center, is a battalion of angels. Once, I would have stood with them, prepared for a battle I'd itch for, thinking I was doing the right thing. They shine brightly in the moonlight from the opening above, lighting up their runes. Their weapons glow with angel dust and power, and they stand, cold and ready, waiting for orders.

I would have been a noble little warrior like them, just following orders.

It strikes me then that they may be no more aware of whom they are following than I was. They don't know this war or the seraphim's true intentions. They don't know we were all lied to.

Maybe there is time to stop this yet.

Gathering my courage, I begin to push through the ranks, the demons parting for me and creating a tunnel to my mate who waits with his hand out. As soon as I am close enough, I lay mine in his and stand at his side. The hellhounds wrap around me, hissing at the angels who are only feet away before winding down and plopping at my feet, as if they are protecting me.

Vetris looks down and glares at them. "Traitors."

Grinning up at him for a moment, I lose myself in his fire, thinking about how lucky I am before clearing my throat and focusing back on the angels. Long gone are the days of my silence and servitude. It took my whole world changing, it took Vetris, for me to see the truth. Maybe I can do that for them too.

"Yes," I declare. "Mates."

"Impossible," Rael spits.

I turn my glare on him. "I wasn't talking to you, fuckwit."

"That's my girl." Vetris laughs.

Ignoring the bulging eyes and veins throbbing in the seraphim's face, I focus back on the army of angels, hoping to reach at least a few of them and show them who the real enemy is.

"Yes, we are mates. Everything we thought we knew is a lie. Demons and angels can be mates. Hell, they have been before, but it's more than that. I am not your enemy. You know this. I trained with you. I fought at your side. You know me. I would have died for my people, for the angels, but it wasn't enough. They didn't just want my death, they wanted my soul. They wanted to ruin who I was and use it. I'm innocent. The only crime I committed was being too trusting." Vetris squeezes my hand, supporting me as my voice rings out for everyone to hear. Maybe I always knew this would lead here, but I wouldn't change one thing.

"Are you really ready to risk everything? Your life, your honor, for this seraphim? One who brought you here for lies and deception?" I call to the mass of angels. Some I call friends, and some I have fought side by side with. They shift with unease, while those who never liked me bare their teeth.

"It is not in our duty to question the seraphim. We do as we are ordered. It is our holy light," one of the angels retorts, but there's a thread of hesitation in his voice that I latch onto.

"No, it's a way to keep you contained and pliant so you are useless guard dogs following him around and increasing his power. He stands here before you, filled with anger and lies. You are the ones attacking Soleil. You came into their home and threatened their families, mates, and children. You are the bad guys here, not the demons who took me in when my own people turned on me, imprisoned me, and tried to kill me for no reason other than it suited them. The demons' only crime is watching their prince fall in love with a fallen angel." Looking up at Vetris, I speak nothing but the truth. "My only crime is loving you, and I will gladly live with that." His eyes fill with emotion that nearly takes me out, but there are more words I need to say. Looking back at the angels, I tilt my chin up. "If you really want this war and want to follow orders blindly, then you have it. I will not let you hurt my mate. I will not let you destroy this home. You will bathe in our hellfire alongside your leader. It is your choice. Peace or war?"

For a moment, nothing happens. I see some of their weapons droop in uncertainty, and hope blooms inside me, but then Rael's voice cuts through the peace. "War! You will be stripped of your wings and then your life for your treachery! For Celestia!" he roars, and the weapons come back up. The orders bolt them to the spot, to their destiny.

At least I tried, I think as I reach for my weapon, ready to fight and die alongside my mate.

I feel Vetris vibrate next to me. "Then come and get it, angel scum," he taunts. "Soleil, let's give them hell!"

A battle cry goes up among the demons, unnerving some of the angels, so I add my voice in, and when it quiets down, we are prepared to charge.

"Oh no you fucking don't! You aren't starting this war without me!" comes a familiar voice, and we all turn to see Abraxos striding through the masses and reaching our sides. He winks at me, clutching two large rapiers in his hands. "I've been dreaming of the day I would get to taste angel blood for what they did to me and for what they took from me." He faces forward again. "For my mate!" With a mighty roar, he charges the angels, his wings tucked in tight against his back. Vetris and I share a look before roaring our own challenge and flying at the waiting army.

The clash of swords is loud.

The death cries begin.

My mate and I fly toward our destiny.

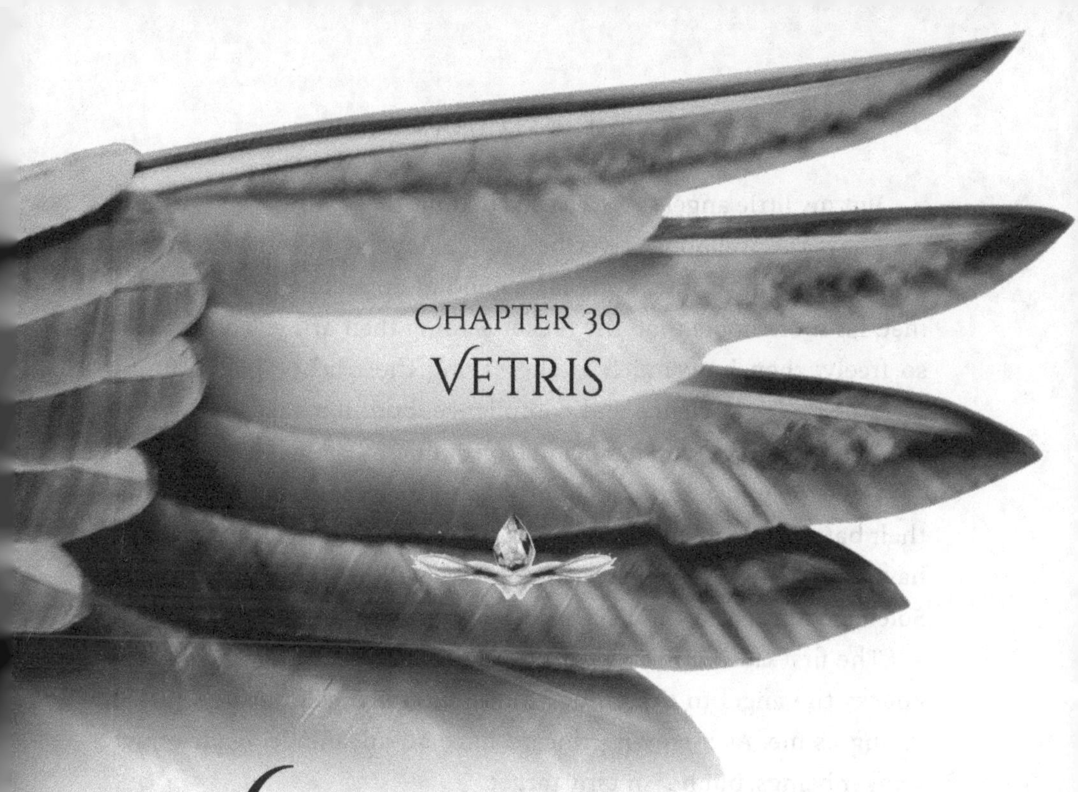

CHAPTER 30
VETRIS

War is a terrible thing.

Death feasts on both sides, and all for what? For ego. For power. For ridiculous notions of grandeur and lies. One side wins, but at a cost that usually feels too great. The last war between Soleil and Celestia was because of ego.

This one is for love.

The fiery archangel at my side looks at me with love despite our differences, and I would burn all the realms for her. Luckily for me, I don't have to.

I only have to burn down one.

With battle cries that shake the underground, we launch into war that derived from a single seraphim's lies. There are eight of them, just as there are eight princes, but Rael has been a fucking thorn in my side for as long as we've both been alive. He is a greedy angel who pretends to be holy, just, fair, and gentle when he's anything but. Today, that seraphim wears his golden, glittering armor as if he's some noble motherfucker intent on spreading holy retribution.

But my little angel sowed a seed of doubt.

I saw the weapons lower before Rael spoke. I saw their hesitation. Not all, but some. Roux is as good of an archangel as I've ever met, far more noble than the fucker leading their army. If she speaks so freely, then how much is she saying the truth? Their training dictates their obedience and compliance, but all it takes is a single seed to watch that worship begin to crumble.

My people rush forward alongside us, their faces split into snarls, their battle cries as loud as my own. We have known unfair wars, we have experienced terrible deaths, and we will never stop fighting for Soleil, no matter how much the angels target us.

The first clash of my sword sends a ricochet through the air that knocks the angel to the ground. He's an archangel, but he's not as strong as me. As a crown prince, I have an advantage against such weaker beings, but he isn't my target.

"Stay down and you will live," I snarl, prepared to step over him and save his life.

I do it for Roux, who battles just as fiercely beside me. She wears no armor—we had no time to have some made—but she doesn't need it. She's covered her body in weapons, and metal glints from every available space. She swings her smaller sword, cutting down angels who come after her for her seeds of doubt. Hellfire clings to her shoulders and climbs along the sword in a way that shouldn't be possible. I have no true knowledge of what a demon and an angel mate can accomplish, but as that hellfire burns and claws at the angels she touches, I have to wonder how much stronger we will become. Abraxos spoke of it like a dirty secret, but this is still new. We've barely accepted the mating.

How brightly will we burn once it fully sets in?

The angel at my feet snarls and springs up, ready to stab his sword through my abdomen. I sigh, not because I care for this angel, but because Roux will. Each and every angel death will hurt her, and she will blame herself even though there's only a single angel to blame—the motherfucker standing at the back of warriors, watching rather than joining in.

Coward.

Saying a silent apology for the pain I'm going to bring Roux later, I flick a speck of hellfire at the angel, grimacing when it begins to burn him from the edges of his wings in. It's a painful death, one I wouldn't wish on anyone, but it's effective.

Roux and I seem to be the angry angels' targets, either because of their resentment or because Rael ordered it. I don't know which. Either way, we're surrounded by angels. My brothers and sister move in close, fighting in a line with us, taking down angel after angel. Our people battle on the sides, taking out angels with their numbers though many of them are weaker than the battalion. Pride fills me at their fortitude, at their strength. Celestia can never hope to inspire such passion and power. Not all of their people are warriors, but every single one of mine is.

The sounds of hellhounds baying in battle has me glancing over at my mate, where they cluster around her. At some point, the beasts must have decided that she is their master because they surround her, tearing into angels as they get too close. I've never been able to get them to listen to me in that way, but this is different. Roux isn't commanding them. She's just existing, and they are choosing to exist with her. She's earned their respect through being and nothing more.

My mate is meant for this.

I'm so focused on her, I almost miss the sword swinging toward my neck.

Almost.

I snarl and duck, ramming my massive sword through the middle of the angel and splitting her in two while lifting her into the air. Her screech threatens to make my ears bleed, but I can't focus on that right now. We're in a fight for our lives. Yanking my sword free, I watch her crumple to the ground, her life snuffed out, and all I can think is how pointless their deaths are.

As a demon, we revel in pain and bloodshed, but I wish I was back with my angel in bed, enjoying our new bond. Not here, splattered with the blood of my enemies, staining my soul and sword as I carve a path toward a traitor.

We're making good work of their numbers, cutting them down. The seraphim linger in the back, afraid to fight, but not afraid to sacrifice their people for petty games. I snap my wings wide, calling attention to myself, and when Rael looks over at me, I point my sword at him just before I cut down two more of his warriors. Archangels are no match for eight princes and the demons of Soleil.

Fear flickers in Rael's eyes, fear that gives me great satisfaction. I hope that fear remains when I reach him, and I hope it reflects back at him as I slice his wings from his body.

In a move I don't expect, Rael calls to his people. "To the wastelands! Spread your wings and fight in the skies!"

Snarling at the angels suddenly taking flight, I check to make sure Roux is okay before arrowing into the air after them. They have realized the error of their ways in attacking Soleil on our level. We have the advantage here. In the skies, they think they do.

"Cowards," Roux spits, appearing beside me, flapping her blood splattered wings while the hounds bay sadly from below, trying to reach her. "They know we're winning."

Going to wastelands will give them an advantage, since not all demons have wings, and those without will have to climb the flights of stairs up to the wastelands. The hellhounds are already baying and running at the loss of Roux, their speed bringing them up the stairs faster than the demons. Those of us with wings take to the skies after the angels. My hellfire dances across my skin and jumps between Roux and me as we soar. She looks every inch the battle angel, beautiful and vengeful.

We both shoot up from the main opening to Soleil together, our wingtips touching with an intimacy that makes me yearn for the post-battle sex I know we'll have, but that's still far enough away. I must focus on the angels above us.

Arrows rain down on us, bouncing off of armor and burning up when they hit hellfire, but it takes down some of the lower demons flying with us. We're faster than they prepare for, however, because the archers are targeted a few seconds later, and my family and I make quick work of the gaggle of idiots still trying to load their bows with another arrow.

Angels and demons alike rain down around us.

"This is fucking stupid," Roux snarls, cutting down another angel she might have called a friend. She doesn't let her emotions show, but I can tell it's killing her. She's strong, but my angel wears her heart on her sleeve most of the time. It is taking everything she has to steel herself against this horror. "We need to stop it before their entire side is gone. I refuse to let one fool wipe out my entire race." She glances at Rael. "We take him out. We can convince the others to stop. Cut off the head of the snake, and the others will stop."

I nod. "We'll take him out." I know I'll have to be the one who takes him out. Roux is strong, but I don't know if she's strong enough to take out a seraphim. Together, perhaps, we can make it quick work. "We cut our way—"

Before I can finish my sentence, an angel comes out of nowhere, barreling shoulder first into my unicorn. It knocks her breath from her lungs and sends her sword careening down to the wasteland below us. Hopefully it doesn't spear some poor demon digging its way up from Soleil. I immediately change courses to go help her, but before I can, three angels surround me.

I raise my brow. "Wrong move, pigeons." I swing my sword.

Even as I enter a battle of my own, I keep my eye on Roux. I trust in her strength and know she can fight, but fear still fills me as the sight of her sword falling flashes in my mind. Her and the other angel plummet after the weapon, and at the last minute, they both break apart and land whole on the ground beneath us.

Relief fills me.

"I don't have time for this. My fucking mate needs me," I snarl at the angels around me. I push at the hellfire inside me, and with energy I don't usually expend, I push it outward. It slams into all three angels, burning them to a crisp, before slamming back into me in a move that leaves me breathless. I don't care. I fold my wings and plummet toward the wastelands, hoping I'm not too late. I land on the ground so hard it churns up the dust around me, my fist hitting the earth the same time as one knee does. My wings are spread wide around me, their inky feathers intertwined with glinting metal. I stand just as Roux faces off with this warrior angel I don't know.

Roux grins, and I watch as she pulls a length of chain from her side and drops it to the ground, her fingers holding one end and the sharp blade of the other digging into the dirt.

"Oh, I've been waiting for this," Roux purrs, and my brows rise in surprise.

Hellfire begins to dance at her feet, coming up from Soleil, and climbs along her legs. In a display I've never seen before from a demon, and certainly not an angel, the hellfire climbs her body, lights her on fire, and travels along the chain, making her weapon even more deadly.

Growls fill the air as hellhounds appear out of the underground, their snarls revealing sharp teeth dripping with angel blood and saliva. Two, four, twelve hellhounds come to her side, surrounding her, offering protection and power. With a grin, Roux stands before them.

The sight of my angel lit by my hellfire and standing with my hounds nearly takes me out. She looks like the fallen angel of nightmares, so much so that this general takes a step back.

Rightly so.

"You get him, mate," I call, practically cheering. "Show that fucker who's boss."

With a wink in my direction, Roux swings that chain around, and I fall a little more in love with her.

"Fucking hell, I love that angel," I whisper to myself before I swing my own sword at the angels who dare to target the crown prince.

Hellfire dances around us.
Demon and angel.
Lovers.
Mates.
The ground beneath our feet begins to shake.

CHAPTER 31
ROUX

My old commander, Ajop, hesitates only for a moment, but that moment tells me he's not sure about who will win.

I am. I will win, I have to. I have a mate to protect and a war to win, and no one will get in my way. Every second we delay is another second filled with death on both sides. We need to finish this, and now all that stands in my way is the gruff angel who always hated me.

This will be too easy.

For a moment, I glance at Vetris who spins, his sword cleaving angels in half. He's covered in the blood of my old people, and he wears a sarcastic grin on his face as hellfire dances across his skin, and it's then I realize I've never been more in love. I know he hates angels, and a lot of them probably secretly want this war, but not my love. No matter what he says, he wouldn't want to risk his people, still scarred from the last war. It's another piece of motivation to finish this and finish this quickly.

The sun shines down on us, the shafts of brightness highlighting our angel runes which flare brighter at the other's presence. Ajop's mouth twists in a sneer. "You could never best me in training. You will not do so here. You always were a weak archangel."

"And you were always an asshole." I grin, flipping my chain in an arc. "Enough talking, even if it's all you're good for." I leap into action, making the first move, knowing he won't expect that.

We clash in the air, my chain slashing his side as his sword cuts through mine, and then we fall back before circling each other. Each jab, each movement is too easy to predict. We have fought together too many times, so we know each other's patterns. It makes it an even match.

I swoop to the left, and he blocks. He feints right and moves left, and I match him, knowing that move. Finally, we are simply dancing, not landing a hit as the war continues around us. Death cries fill the air, and blood soaks into the ground once more, until I lose focus for a second, searching for Vetris, and Ajop's sword smacks into my face, sending me tumbling to the ground. I leap to my feet, prodding my aching nose. Blood drips from it and my lips as he chuckles and flutters above me in the air.

"So weak and sentimental. It always was your failure, angel."

Angel, because that's what he sees me as despite the hellhounds at my side ripping into those who get too close and the hellfire licking at my boots. He still sees me as that lowly archangel he was in charge of.

That's when I realize I'm still fighting like an angel, not a fallen angel and the mate of the crown prince. It's time to change that.

I focus on the hellfire dancing at my feet and the heat that never burns me. I pull it upward, coaxing it along my body, urging it to help me. Surprisingly, it listens, until my runes are alight with hellfire instead of the sun, and the flames lick at my arms and pool into my hands. Grinning, I focus on the commander, and with a snarl, I throw the collected hellfire at him.

Surprise flickers in his eyes, and there's fear there too. I like that look a little too much. As he falls back from the hellfire, I advance, changing the tide of this small battle.

I spin the chain, gaining momentum as the hellfire grows larger along it. The chain slices through the air and wraps around his neck, his face turning ashen and then red as the hellfire crawls along it, heating up the chain as I drag him closer despite his flapping wings. When he's just before me, his face dripping with fear, I bare my teeth.

"I'm not just an angel. I'm a fallen fucking angel, you pompous prick." I slam my head into his, and he crumples to the ground, but I still don't stop. I could walk away now, but he would sink a dagger into my or Vetris's back the first chance he got. No, he's one of the best warriors here. I will not let another fall under his greedy sword, so I tighten the chain and drag him to his knees. As he watches the fire crawl closer and closer, he begins to struggle, his wings flapping and muscles straining.

"Fuck you!" he roars.

"Not very angelic, is it?" I sneer.

"You stupid demon slut—" He screams as the loop around his neck is consumed by flames, and I watch with rapt curiosity as it burns through his flesh, the chain popping free. Spinning, I slam my wings into his head, watching it fly off his body and through the air.

"Asshole," I mutter as I loop the chain around my hand and turn back to the fight. Vetris is engaged with five others, and I'm about to go help him when a cry splits the air. I glance over to see a group of angels charging me. I drop into my fighting stance, but they don't even spare me a glance as they race past.

Abraxos sprints past me, chasing the running angels, his hoots filling the air. "Get back here, you fucking cowards. I want to taste your angelic blood."

Well, okay then.

I duck a blade and turn to slash the chain through the angel's body, not bothering to watch them fall as I jog over to my sword. I'm just reaching for it when an ax comes down on it, blocking me. I stumble back and bring up my chain, but one of the hellhounds beats me to it. Leaping at the angel, the hound takes him down to the ground and tears into his body. His screams fill the air as I pick up my sword and swing it, making sure to avoid the hound. I end the angel's life quickly and pet the bloodied hound as a thank you.

"Good boy, yes you are, such a good boy," I coo as I throw a knife at an angel attempting to sneak up on me. I don't even bother to watch it pierce his neck. "Yes you are, now let's go get your daddy."

Lifting my head, I search for Vetris again, but my heart clenches at the destruction around us. The sand is turning red and muddy with blood, and bodies pile upon bodies, angels and demons alike, their faces frozen in terror. The clashing armies clamber over them like they are nothing more than a nuisance.

There is so much death.

The horns of hell sound as demons pour from the hole and angels come down from the sky, and I know that if this continues, neither of our races will win. There will only be more death.

"Roux, duck!" Vetris yells, and I immediately flatten to the ground, lifting my head to see his sword flying through the air and slicing through an angel sneaking up on me. Spinning to my feet, I grab the crossbow and aim behind him. He stands still as I fire, and it flies past him to impale an angel climbing to his feet behind him.

The sun suddenly disappears, blotting out the sky, as the ground trembles and cracks open. Beings—no, creatures begin shooting from the depths of the earth and soar high into the sky. Angels start to take flight, trying to get away, while demons stumble and stare in awe.

"What are they?" I call to Vetris as he rolls over an angel's back while slicing his neck. Tossing his hair back, he wanders over to me, spinning his blade. His eyes greedily drink me in, noticing every small wound and growling with anger when he finds one. "Vetris," I demand.

His eyes follow my finger, and he begins to laugh.

The sound is full-bellied and slightly insane.

"Those, mate, are the creatures from the deep. They come from the very depths of hell themselves and haven't been seen since the last war. They are Titans."

Oh shit.

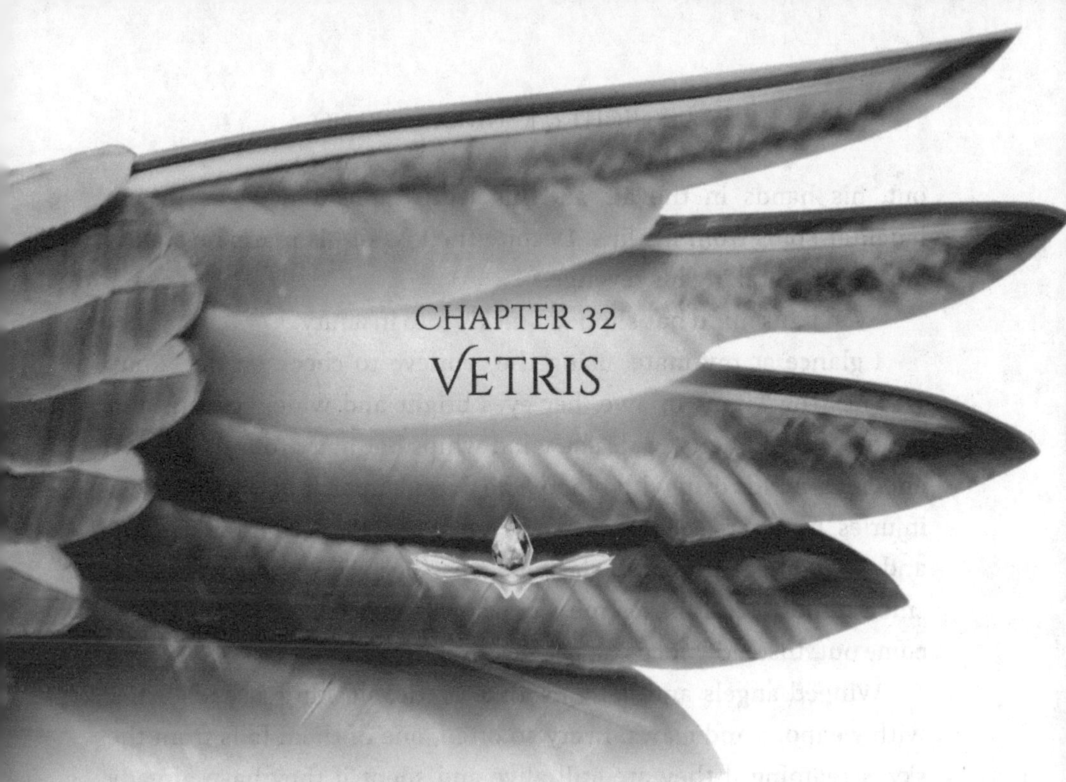

CHAPTER 32
VETRIS

I haven't seen the Titans in so long, I almost forgot what they look like. Large and brutal in appearance, the Titans are far more intimidating than the hordes of demons still rushing up from Soleil. As elemental creatures born of hellfire, the flames race under their hard, rock-colored skin like lava. They have dark pits for eyes, lit with the fires of hell, and their rock mouths are open in a war cry. The jagged edges of their bodies lift as they surge forward.

They immediately go for the angels in the sky, arrowing toward them on wings so large it seems like it would be impossible for them to fly. Many of them are less humanoid than most demons, their faces reminiscent of various earthen creatures. They aren't strategists, but Titans don't need to be. Their sheer numbers and aggression are what make them a threat. Kill one, and three more take its place. Apparently, the sight of them pouring from the deep is too much for the angels, and many of them begin to flee.

I watch as a massive, bear-shaped Titan smashes its rock fist through a fleeing crowd of two dozen angels, and they fall to the ground like broken insects as it roars in victory.

Abraxos stands on the edge of the fissure where the Titans pour out, his hands in the air and his wings spread wide as insane laughter spills from his lips. Despite the loss of his mate, he stands here with us, taking his revenge.

Even if his mind has slipped quickly into insanity.

I glance at my mate, using the reprieve to check on her. Roux watches the Titans in awe, her eyes bright and wide, accepting of another part of her world. The wind whips her hair around her face, and her wounds drip with blood. She doesn't appear bothered by her injuries, but there is a large gash in her side, her nose and lips bleed, and there are a few more slashes across her arms and thighs. The smell of her blood makes me vicious, a savage creature wanting to come out. Instead, I focus on the war above us.

Winged angels and demons alike battle, slashing at each other with weapons and claws. Every so often, one of them falls from the sky, screaming if they are still alive and silent if they have already been cut down. More bodies pile up around us, the earth awash with blood. I haven't seen it look like this since the last war, and all for a seraphim's stupid whims.

"We have to take him out," I snarl, searching through the chaos for the seraphim on the edges of battle, surrounded by archangels willing to die to protect him. "We need to do it now."

Roux nods. "Too many are dying." She looks over at me, and I see the knowledge in her eyes that she knows she isn't strong enough to fight a seraphim, even if I am.

The thought that she could die before we've really gotten a chance to live makes me want to bare my teeth.

"I'll distract the angels protecting him, while you take out Rael." She spreads her wings, prepared to take flight, but I grab her wrist before she can do so, and her eyes meet mine. "What is it?"

"You're going to live, unicorn," I growl. "And if you die, I'm going to be extremely pissed. I will drag your fucking soul back and trap it in hell with me."

"Likewise, princess," she teases and moves to fly again, but I hold her back.

"I'm serious, Roux. If you die, I will burn Celestia to the ground." The hellfire along my shoulders brightens. "There will be no survivors. I will make them all pay for the loss of the single bit of sunshine in my life, and then I will join you in the beyond."

Her face softens, and she wraps her arms around me, holding me tightly. "You will not decimate an entire realm for me, Vetris."

"I will."

"No," she says, leaning back to meet my eyes. "I'm asking you not to."

I blink down at her. "You'd ask me to suffer from knowing your killers are still out there?"

She shakes her head. "No, I'm asking you not to kill innocent angels when there's only one to blame for all of this. Regardless, I don't plan on dying." She cups my cheek. "Let's finish this before any more of our people die."

When she says *our people*, I realize she doesn't just mean the demons fighting amongst us. She means the archangels fighting, running, and screaming. They are afraid of defying the seraphim. They are afraid of what their conditioning has taught them. They are afraid of the Titans, Roux, and me.

They are afraid of the truth, but fear is a hell of a motivator.

"I love you," I tell Roux, dragging her in for a gentle kiss. The declaration fills the sky with a promise of forever. Her nose is probably broken, judging by the blood, but when she realizes I'm avoiding it, she reaches up and cracks it back into place with a wince. "Hellfire, I love the fuck out of you," I tell her again, pressing my forehead against hers. "If we don't get enough time in this life, I'm going to find you in the next."

She smiles. "And I will search for you in every lifetime until you're in my arms again. I love you, Vetris." She sighs. "Now, let's go kill a seraphim."

Knowing we can't linger in this moment forever, I press another kiss to her forehead and step back, giving us both enough room to spread our wings.

As she stands there, waiting for my cue, I realize I've long since forgiven Celestia for their crimes and for following a mad angel.

I forgive them because they had her.

"For this life," I tell her gently, taking in every detail of my warrior, my angel, my mate.

"And all those that come after." She nods, dropping her chain. "Until the very end."

Then we take to the skies together.

CHAPTER 33
ROUX

In this life or the next. His words ring through my head, but I can't focus on them. We both have a job to do, and I can't let fear win. Instead, I harness it as I spiral toward the angels protecting the coward—my one job in this battle. I focus on it entirely as Vetris swoops away to circle the seraphim and get behind him. I use my chain as I fly higher and higher, slashing at the angels until they surge after me, soaring down toward the ground as I pretend to flee, feet away from the seraphim where only a few angels remain at his side. Most of the other angels follow his barked scream to kill me, not noticing Vetris gaining ground behind him.

For a moment, I meet my mate's eyes, but then I jerk my gaze away as a sword swings violently toward my waist.

I manage to dive under it and come up fighting, wrapping the chain around his throat as I move. With a yell of anger, I throw myself back, spinning through the air to pull his head off. It twists through the air as I yank the chain back and use it like a hammer, beating those who surge closer. A circle closes around me, caging me in and stealing my ability to move with a wider arc. My eyes are hard, my mouth set in determination as I whip around, taking out angel after angel, beings I used to call friends, comrades, and family.

"Come on, you angelic bastards! Is that all you've got?" I yell, keeping their attention on me and not on my mate. I have no choice but to fight from that moment on. Their anger is palpable, as is their confusion. I fight for my life, for my future, for my mate.

I can barely breathe, and my heart thunders as I face insurmountable odds.

I knock out some and kill others, but another takes their place the moment one falls. No matter how much traction I seem to gain, I also lose some, until I just fight without knowing when it will end. Keeping the chain loose in one hand, I use it like a shield to keep others back as I clash swords with another angel. His sneering, blood-coated face peers through our crossed swords, so I smash my head into his, watching him tumble back as I bounce forward again, stabbing my sword through his chest and spinning to pull my blade free. All the while, I lash out with the hellfire chain, clothes burning and angels screaming from the power that fills me.

I dance, swing, and move.

The hellhounds find me and join the battle, giving me some leeway even as I fight with brutal focus. There are so many angels attacking me, I barely know where they begin and end.

I keep moving, knowing movement is life and Vetris is depending on me to survive. I will not fail my mate. Not now. All my training has led to this as my mind blanks and I fall back into my center. The angels around me blot out sight of anything else, their brightly colored wings high in the air. I don't know if we are winning. I don't know if Vetris is close, or even alive, but I have to trust him.

Gritting my teeth against sudden agony that tears through my wings, I bring them close to my body, and with a savage yell, I slam them back out. Power flows through them, and the strength of it mixed with the force of my wings sends a whole wall of angels scattering back, and that's when I see Vetris. He's close to the seraphim, his sword raised high and his face filled with fury. The seraphim is pale and backing away, but Vetris is so focused on his task, my mate doesn't see the angel sneaking up on him. His would-be assailant is missing one arm, but he holds a sword in the other.

A sword that can cleave my mate in two.

Instinct takes hold of me, and with a roar, I flip my sword and throw it through the air with every bit of strength I possess. I watch it sail through the madness of battle and sink home, spearing the angel behind Vetris and sending him spiraling away from my mate. Vetris glances over his shoulder, wide-eyed, and then back to me. He hesitates, looking at the angels moving toward me, so I smile, knowing it's bloody but happy.

"Keep going!" I yell, and then the angels surge around me, blocking him from view. There's a whole swarm of them, and all I have left is my chain. I swing it with all my might, filling it with my power and the hellfire I'd been gifted by Vetris. I take as many of them out as I can, knowing if I'm going to die, I'm going to take as many of them with me as possible. Leaping into the air, I swing the chain under my legs, ripping two angels apart before spinning left and slicing through more. I move like air, sure and strong, never stopping and never giving up. Even when I feel hands on me and blades slicing through my flesh, I don't stop, not until the crowd gets too big. Somewhere in it, my chain is trapped and thrown away, leaving me defenseless.

Or so they think.

It still doesn't stop me. The scent of burning flesh and blood fills the air, and the screams of battle fill my head as I kick and punch, hellfire leaving its mark. I infuse every hit with my power, tapping into my reserves and giving it my all, knowing I will need to.

My body aches and begins to slow, and my runes begin to flicker and die out from the power I'm using.

I know I'm not going to make it, even with the hellhounds ripping apart those around them.

I have to give Vetris the best shot he can before they take me, so I bend down, curling around myself as hands claw at me. I let them get as close as they can, tearing at my hair and feathers. All the while, I draw my power from deep inside, letting it build. I wait until I have it all before I let it burst from me, my arms flying out as I scream.

I fall to my knees, and when my vision returns, I find angels scattered everywhere. I start to fall sideways as my sight blackens at the edges, when angels surge back around me and take me down.

I don't resist. I can't fight anymore.

I prepare for the fall of the final blade...

Suddenly, the angel before me falls back, followed by another. A pale hand thrusts through the masses and yanks me out, and I stumble to my knees. The sun blinds me for a moment, and I blink, lifting my head slowly.

When I see who stands before me, I gape.

Rosa shines brightly, her body encased in ornate red and black armor as her hellfire-colored hair flows in the wind. Her eyes are bright with power and destiny, and a bright pink scar runs across her face now, but it only adds to her magnificence. Standing at her side in matching armor is a demon burning with hellfire. He nods at me and fights off the angels coming for us.

"No time to talk," she says quickly. "You need to recharge." She grasps my shoulder and forces her power through it.

Her power smacks into me, and like reigniting a candle, I am filled with power once more. I am not as strong as I usually am, but it's enough for me to get me to my feet and grip the weapon she thrusts at me.

"Rosa," I rasp.

She grins, pulling at the ragged scar on her face, which I can tell was done with an angelic weapon. They tried to kill her, yet she survived somehow, and once again, she is saving me. This time, though, I stand at her side, spinning to face an angel who's sneaking up on her.

"Traitor," he roars at her.

She flips him off, and the demon at her side surges into the chaos with her, both of them glowing with power... and love. It seems I am not the only one who found my destiny.

"Get to your mate," Rosa calls. "I saved you to finish this, Roux. This was always your destiny. Go, I've got this." She turns back to the people who degraded, judged, and hurt her and smiles. "It's time to show you what an angel with hellfire can do."

I hesitate, but I know she's right. I run through the masses, taking down as many as I can, and then I slide to a stop when I see Vetris.

The seraphim's sword is against his neck, and he is on his knees before him, his eyes burning with hatred as he kneels at the seraphim's mercy. Pure panic fills me, and my power flares in response, the likes of which I've never known.

"Vetris!" I scream.

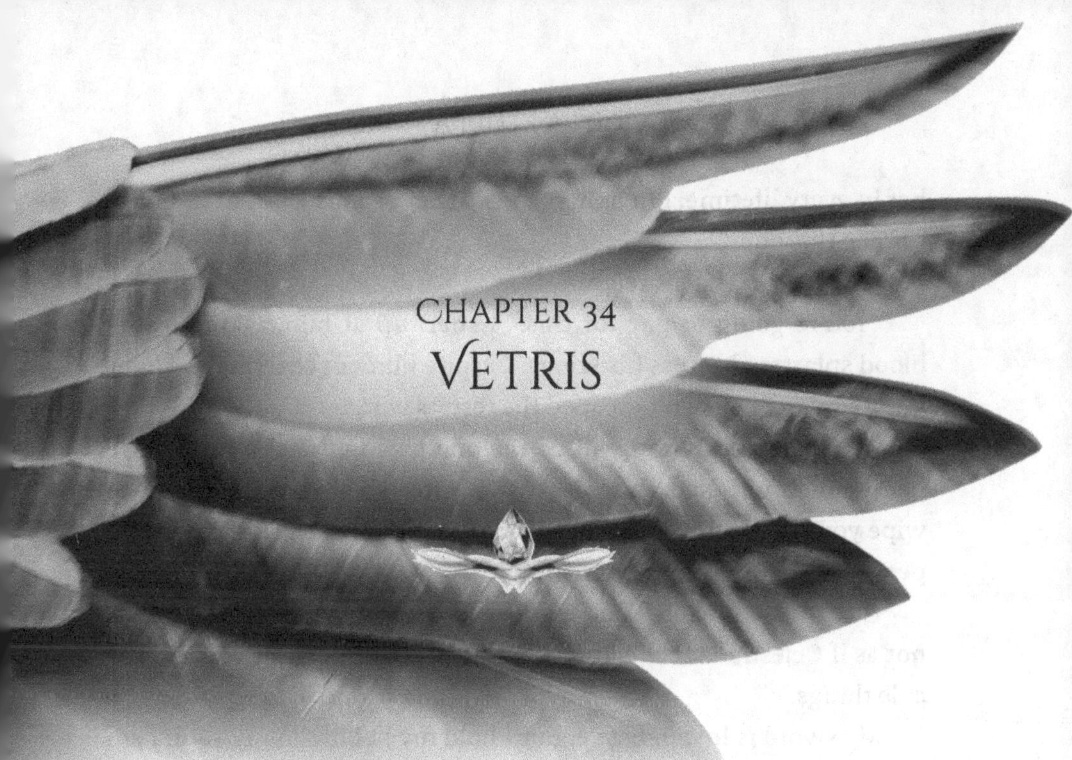

CHAPTER 34
VETRIS

I'm a strong fighter, and I've always been skilled with a sword. I spent many years of my life honing that skill and felled many angels in the last war with the blade I carried into battle—the same blade I carry now. However, the emotions running through me right now are a weakness.

I saw the look in her eyes as she'd been swarmed by angels, keeping them distracted long enough for me to finish the job, but I wasn't prepared for the pain that look would bring, demanding I go after her.

My instincts war between duty and love.

Because of that momentary panic, though, I allow the seraphim to gain the upper hand, and he knocks my sword from my hands and forces me to my knees. I kneel before no one but my mate, and so this angel, this asshole, will pay for this.

I can't see her. The throng of angels fighting against her is large, although the mass of bodies she leaves in her wake is even larger. Pride fills me at her strength, at her ability to keep fighting against so many for so long, but it will be her end. I meant it when I said I'll find her in every lifetime. I'm going to keep that promise, but first, I have to keep this one.

I have to end Rael's reign.

"You're going to pay for this," I snarl up at him, taking in the blood splattered across his wings. Despite him not entering the fight like a coward, he hasn't escaped the results of it.

"It appears as if you will be the one paying," Rael retorts. "I've had enough of Soleil and your ways. After I kill you, I'm going to wipe your city out of existence, and then finally, Celestia can live in peace."

He speaks as if Soleil has spent years attacking the city in the sky, not as if Celestia is the realm who always comes for war over miniscule things.

My sword is lost in battle, but I hold my hellfire in my soul. I am not as helpless as the seraphim thinks, but in order to kill him, I'll need to let him stab his sword through me first, so I can plant my hands on his skin and burn him from the inside out. Before any of that can come to pass, though, I hear my angel.

"Vetris!"

The scream is pure terror, undercut with fury, and both Rael and I turn at the same time, searching for the source of so much emotion.

I find her.

Through the crowd and death, I find her...

She's bloody and wounded, and her wings are missing chunks. Blood runs down her face like a river, and her beautiful orange hair is now stained darker by it. Not a single inch of her body has been spared, but her eyes are bright with fury, demanding vengeance. She sees me on my knees and explodes forward, holding no weapons except for a single, weaker angel blade. Hellfire dances along her shoulders and trails in her wake, the hellhounds who have lasted through battle are on her heels, their teeth dripping with angel blood.

She's like a picture, all avenging fallen angel, and I mentally take in every detail so I can have a Soleil artist paint it for me later, an image I want hanging in my throne room for all to see.

The strength, power, and determination of my mate.

Her beauty is unrivaled.

Despite having a blade against my neck, I'm mesmerized by the sight as she flies forward on wings that shouldn't work.

The closer she gets, the more I can feel the sheer power flowing through her. My eyes widen at the strength of it and the way it coats my throat and stings.

Angelic and demonic power coexist in one body, stronger than both.

"You. Will. Not. Touch. My. Mate!" she snarls, the sound more animal than angel. Long gone is the pristine angel I hunted down on Earth. Long gone is the angel concerned with earning her way back into Celestia.

This is a woman hellbent on changing the world, and I'm going to be right there beside her as she does it.

The seraphim, sensing this new threat, turns toward her rather than focusing on me, and I see the chance to take his life, but this isn't my kill to make. We'd been mistaken. It was never my job. It was hers. It's always been hers.

I drag myself to my feet, my wounds as great as hers, and with a savage snarl, I lean forward.

"Go to hell," I hiss, just before I shove the seraphim forward toward my mate.

Her power explodes out of her in a bright blaze that makes me close my eyes. The hellfire and angelic powers come out as a single entity, slamming into the seraphim with the force of a storm, consuming him.

She screams, I scream, and the seraphim screams in agony as the power burns him. His skin begins to flake off, disintegrating into the air. The fighting around us stops as they all take in the sight of the seraphim clawing at his face and eyes, begging for mercy.

But we've long since run out of mercy.

His runes light up, burning from within with Roux's hellfire, taking everything he has to give, and then, with a final shrill shriek of my mate, he explodes outward, splintering apart from the power. Angel dust begins to rain down on us, glittering in a mocking display of pretty sparkles. It lands on the death at our feet, leaving corpses with a shine they should never have. Angels gape in horror as my mate stands before the destruction of their seraphim, an archangel who shouldn't have been able to kill him. She's panting, her eyes focused on where he used to be, and then I see her hellfire flicker out.

With a curse, I lurch forward just as she starts to sway.

"Oh no you don't," I chide her as I offer what little strength I still have. We both stumble before righting ourselves. We lean heavily against each other, sharing strength. She can have it all. She can have every drop of my life force. "We're not finished, unicorn."

With a sigh, she lifts her head slowly and stares at the angels who stopped, their weapons drooping and eyes wide. The demons, my own people, stare at her the same way, watching her with rapt attention. No one is fighting anymore after Rael literally exploded before them, killed by an archangel—something that shouldn't have been possible. Each and every one of them is waiting, as if expecting her to say something. Maybe they are waiting for her to declare them all the enemy.

"Do I have to?" she murmurs, exhaustion in her voice.

I lift her higher and allow her to raise her chin. "Let them see the truth, Roux. Let them see your strength."

With the willpower of a goddess, my mate raises her head, her fingers tightening in mine before she takes a deep breath and begins to speak.

CHAPTER 35
ROUX

I tighten my hold on my mate. I will never let him go again. I had come so close to losing him. I saw it happening as if in slow motion, and it brought forth a tidal wave of fury and power, drawn from the very depths of my soul. It was born from the love between us, a demon and angel.

Abraxos was right. We are stronger than both.

After all, I shouldn't have been able to kill a seraphim, my leader, but I did for Vetris, who practically holds me up now. Pride and love shine in his eyes.

His wounds are just as terrible as mine, his hair is drenched with blood, and he has a cut marring the beauty of his face as if they tried to skin him for it. Another jagged one decorates his throat, and I see more across his chest. Some of his feathers are torn free and bleeding, and he almost sways as he holds me up.

We have to finish this now. We have to set the tone for the future before we both pass out.

There is so much death and pain filling the air, the ground almost quivers with it. Angels and demons stand side by side, caught where they were in battle. Pale, glowing faces are streaked with soot and blood, their fire extinguished by the sun and pain. In that moment, we are one people, and I see a vision of what we could be, if only we are strong enough to reach out and take it. Even the Titans wait, holding their breath.

I feel the change in the air.

Our world is waiting for our decision.

Do we damn it, or do we cleanse it and start again?

"You've got this, mate," Vetris murmurs. Clasping my hand tighter, he pushes me to stand up taller.

Nodding, I clear my throat. I'm exhausted, mentally, emotionally, and physically, but he's right. We need to do this now or this will never stop. This has to be the end. We can't sustain this hatred anymore.

With a certainty I feel and a strength I do not, I open my mouth, projecting my voice across the battleground with the last of my power. It's filled with my fear, love, relief, and hope.

The wind carries it farther as if trying to help me.

"Stop this. It is over. The man who ordered this war is done, his demise brought by his own treachery and lies. Do not let his rot fill you anymore. The war is over. There has been enough death and lies between our races and too much hate. It is time to end that." I look at Vetris. "If I, an archangel, can choose to love and trust a crown prince of Soleil and he can choose to love and trust an angel of Celestia, then there is hope for all of us. Do not let the deaths of our friends, lovers, and family members be in vain."

I look back out at the tired and pained faces and see a spark of change and hope.

"Haven't enough died here today? Haven't enough sacrificed their lives for this war, and for what? Nothing will change unless we make it so. Let's create the change we want. We will bury our dead, and with it, we'll bury our differences. From today and all days after, we will be one—one people. No more wars or death. We are joined now through love. Let it bloom. It will not be easy, but it is easier to fight for that every day than to fight for hate. Can you not see we are stronger together?" Whispers ensue as they look at the dust covering my skin. "Leave your weapons and gather the dead. Tonight we mourn and cleanse this ground, then we move on, but we will never forget the lessons we have learned here. Blood and sacrifice will become the building blocks of our new world. We'll do this together, for Celestia and Soleil!"

For a moment, there is nothing but silence, and I worry, until suddenly, thunder explodes—okay, not thunder, but thousands of feet stomping as one. The ground shakes with it as the Titans join in.

"Together for our dead, Celestia, and Soleil!" The call goes up, being carried by the wind.

Weapons drop and shoulders slump as angels and demons turn to one another. Hands are given to those who are struggling, and help is provided to those who need it. Dead angels are carefully carried by demons to the angels, and demons are carried by the angels.

It's hesitant, but it's there. They collect their dead, and the mood turns somber, each worried about what is to come but finally giving into change that has been needed for so long. We watch it happen. We watch the battlefield become a place of death and then one of hope and remembrance.

The angels take to the sky with their dead, and the demons to the ground. After all, change doesn't happen overnight, but the sight will remain with me—demons helping angels and vice versa. Change is upon us, and I am ready for it.

Abraxos appears and salutes me. "Knew you could do it, angel." He glares at Vetris. "I still don't like you." Putting his sword away, he looks around. "This will be a bitch to clean up. If only my demon could see it, she..." He looks back at me, and his face softens. "She would tell me I have just witnessed history—the rebirth of our lands. You did her proud, and so did I, I hope. You can hate me for stealing the orb, but my plan was to create change and possibilities so future generations do not have to feel the loss I have. I guess I just never realized it wouldn't be me who brought about the change." He smiles at us. "Go and rest. You look like shit. Tomorrow is a new day." He begins to walk away, carving a path through the blood-soaked earth. "I have a feeling it's going to be the first of many good ones!" he calls.

Shaking my head, I look up at Vetris. "Take me home?"

"Always, unicorn, always," he replies.

Together, hand in hand, we stumble back into Soleil, paying our respects to those who gave their lives as we go. Once inside our chambers, our weapons hit the floor before we both stumble to the rumpled bed, the hellhounds curling near the flames and doors to protect us.

So much has changed in such a short amount of time, but as I stare at the messy sheets from our lovemaking, I know this was always our destiny.

When we climb into bed, our hands clasped together, both of us fall into a deep healing sleep.

Our powers are drained, and our bodies are exhausted, but our hearts are full with hope for the future and our love for one another.

CHAPTER 36
VETRIS

We sleep for days, our bodies so drained that they need healing only the deepest of magical sleeps can give. Once we wake, there are still wounds that need to mend, such as the ones on our wings and the deep gash along my scalp, but the smaller scrapes and the exhaustion have been taken care of. Not only that, but our powers have also regenerated, sweeping away the ache that comes with using too much. I wake with my mate in my arms, her face pristine in sleep despite the fact we're still covered in grime and blood. Someone came in to deliver food to us, and the hellhounds keep guard, but otherwise, we've been left undisturbed. Soon, we'll have to venture out to see to our people, to see to both people. The other seraphim haven't spoken a word, their fear palpable when Roux killed Rael, but we'll have to speak with them and come to a consensus between our two realms.

Now one realm.

All because of the angel in my arms.

Everything seems quiet around us, too quiet. It makes me feel as if more is coming, but I know that's just the calm after the storm. After the last war, I spent months staring at the wall, waiting for the next shoe to drop as we all waited in Soleil for the angels to appear and decide to wipe us off the face of this realm. We wouldn't have let them, but it would have meant more death. I didn't want it then, and I don't want it now.

"What are you thinking about?" Roux asks groggily as she drags herself from slumber, her eyes barely opening to glance up at me before closing against the light of the hellfire. "You're going to get wrinkles if you furrow your brows so."

"Demons don't get wrinkles," I retort. "We age gracefully."

She snorts and stretches her arms over her head. "Of course you do, old man."

I'm older than her, but we've never discussed it since it hardly matters. We have each other now. I've waited centuries for my mate, a love I never expected to find. Hunger pounds through me at the feel of her soft curves pressing against me, and my cock hardens, but we need comfort and love right now, not wild sex, so I ignore it.

"Come. Let us get cleaned up and go see what's happening."

We spend our time in the shower tending to each other. I use the sponge to lovingly wash her body, cleansing wounds, and then I take my time to clean each of her wings, careful not to harm the injuries that will take weeks to heal. I kiss the one that will scar her wings. Our wings always heal slower than the rest of our body, and neither one of us will be flying anytime soon in case it strains the delicate tendons there.

Once I finish soaping up her body and shampooing her hair, I wash her off and then she takes the sponge from me. She repeats all the same motions, cleaning me so tenderly that it clogs my throat with emotion. Never before has another tended to me after battle. I try hard not to focus on her gentle touches and the way she carefully cleanses my wounds as if I'm something to revere. I've never felt so loved. When she brushes her hands along my feathers to wash them, I harden once more, but now is hardly the time.

Perhaps later, I'll gently worship her in our bed, careful not to damage our wounds further, but we must tend to the realm first and make sure they haven't descended back into war while we were sleeping.

We dress in loose, comfortable clothing that will not irritate the healing process before stepping back into the room. The hellhounds bound up to her, happy to see her awake as they beg for scratches and pets. They practically ignore me.

"Traitors," I growl, reaching for one. It snaps at me, nearly taking off my fingers, and I scowl. "I guess they are your beasts now, unicorn," I tell her.

She only laughs and ruffles the nearest one's ears. "I'll take perfect care of them. Who's a good boy? That's right! You are!"

We open the doors, and we're met by Gerkun, who stands at attention beyond, his eyes brightening at the sight of us whole and awake. "My prince!" he exclaims. "My mistress! Oh, you have been missed! Soleil awaits you!"

Roux looks down at the smaller demon, delight in her eyes that he survived the battle. Clearly, she'd been worried. "Hello, Gerkun," she coos. "Have things been calm?"

"Oh, yes. I haven't gotten used to the angels appearing to help with our wounded, but I'm sure they feel the same about the demons who go to Celestia, and you will never believe what the wasteland looks like!"

He's right. Neither one of us expect it.

As we walk through the streets of Soleil, demons and angels alike mingle and help rebuild. It seems like they truly are giving into peace, and despite old hatreds, they are bridging the gap. They stop and wave at us as we pass. A few of them clap and whistle, and some bow, but many look at my mate as if she's something to be worshiped.

I don't blame them. If I could spend my time on my knees before her, I would remain there forever, worshiping her just as she deserves.

Roux doesn't let it go to her head however. She's gentle with each demon and angel, bowing her head to them and understanding what was sacrificed for this new change.

She is humble, bright, and beautiful, just as an angel should be.

Once we reach the wasteland, I stare in shock at the sight before us. In the days we've been asleep, great progress has been made to clean up. The dead have been prepared for burial rites, taken back to their final resting places or ready for it. Blood still stains the ground in places, and piles of discarded weapons sit around the space, but none of that is what shocks me.

It's the green peeking through the dryness of the wasteland as it starts to give way to the nature that died after the last war.

"It's growing back," Roux chokes out. "It's changing."

"The orb," I murmur. "Abraxos explained it would cause chaos, but in that chaos, perhaps it's returning to its natural state."

She blinks. "We can't exactly call it a wasteland anymore if it is not a wasteland."

"No," I reply, staring at the grass and small plants that are starting to sprout. "No, we'll have to return to calling it the in-between, just like it was before."

In all my years, I never expected for this to be reversed and for it to return to something so beautiful, it will steal my breath when it's whole again. I realize suddenly that the previous war had all been a lie, a setup by the seraphim, to keep us apart and destroy Soleil completely.

The destruction of this area had only been the beginning.

Now, though, those plans are gone, and angels and demons are working together. Above us, demons soar alongside angels, a sight I've never seen before. Celestia is busy with movement, their own preparations taking place. Soon, we'll have to go there and speak to the remaining seraphim, make arrangements, and settle into a true pact. We're only operating on goodwill now, and that's okay, but someday, another angel or demon might decide to change it. It happened once, and it could happen again.

I pull Roux into my side and hold her close. "Look at what you did," I tell her. "Look at what change you've brought about."

"The change *we* brought about," she corrects, smiling up at me.

Everything feels whole and complete in this moment. I have my mate, the love of my existence, an archangel I didn't know I needed. She's everything, and to her, I'm the same. We exist as equals, and we've changed the world around us. It'll be a long road to true balance, but I have no doubt we'll get there.

"I love you," I tell her, pressing a kiss against her lips.

"And I love you," she murmurs, holding on tight. "Until the very end."

I smile. "Until the very end."

We spread our wings, angel and demon, in love, perfect, and at peace, the likes of which this realm has never known.

CHAPTER 37
ROUX

A party in hell, Soleil, is exactly how I imagined it would be. The celebration is in full swing around us. The throne room is filled with every type of demon you can imagine as they drink, dance, fuck, and play games. The party spills out into the streets as the whole realm celebrates.

Tomorrow, we'll meet with the seraphim on neutral ground, in the in-between, to come up with an arrangement, but for tonight we celebrate our win, and in a demon tradition, we celebrate the lives of those we lost. Although they mourn their dead, they prefer a celebration.

I can't help but giggle as Gerkun bowls past in a game they call Toss the Demon, his laughter filling the air. "I love that sound," Vetris murmurs, and when I turn, his heated eyes are on me. He sits upon his throne with his crown on his head, his arms flickering with hellfire. His legs are encased in leather and spread wide—an offering for me, he said.

"What sound?" I ask, leaning into his throne from the matching one he placed next to his—no one even blinked.

"Your laughter. Never in my long life has the sound of laughter made my heart stop, but yours does every time," he murmurs, leaning into me.

"You big softie. I wonder if they know how soppy their crown prince is." I grin.

Gripping my chin, he drags me closer, sliding his hand down to circle my neck, and lust shoots through me as I hold his fiery gaze. "When it comes to you, mate, I'm all hard. Would you like me to prove it?" he purrs.

I swallow my retort, licking my lips as I gaze into his eyes. "Shouldn't you join your celebration? I'm assuming that before I came along, you were quite the partier."

"Only out of boredom. I'm finding that with my angel at my side, I'm never bored."

"Is that right? Maybe I want to party though." I grin, shifting forward to lick his lips. He groans against me, hand tightening on my throat.

"Do not tease, little angel, or I will have you bent over this throne and filled with my cock quicker than you can react," he snarls.

"Promises, promises," I murmur, giving him a quick kiss. His hand relaxes, and I giggle as I yank myself away and get to my feet.

"You know, I still don't like you very much." I smirk as I stand, holding my hand out to him.

"Feeling's mutual, unicorn," he teases, placing his hand in mine. I hoist him up, and he comes willingly. "Now, shall I corrupt my little angel further and teach her how to drink and play like a demon?"

Releasing his hand, I start to walk backwards into the crowd. "You say that like I don't know how to drink," I purr as he stalks after me. "Like I didn't party up in Celestia. Maybe I should teach you demons how to drink like angels." With that, I dart into the crowd while the demons around us laugh.

We spend all night with his people. He does, in fact, teach me how to drink like a demon, and I, an angel, teach him how to play Angel Ball, which quickly becomes a crowd favorite. Before I know it, I'm being carried by demons who are celebrating in our name.

In my name.

As I smile up at the fires of Soleil, I realize one thing.

I'm home.

~

"You're drunk," I grumble, shouldering Vetris's massive weight as he stumbles down the hallway to our chamber, singing at the top of his lungs. It's as cute as it is hilarious.

"Who knew angels could drink so much?" he mutters as I help him walk.

"I tried to warn you. I think your exact words were, 'I am a big, strong demon prince. I can outdrink you glowing bastards,' and now look at you." I laugh, having to stop for a moment to lean against the wall. A hellhound comes trotting up. He looks at Vetris and then at me, as if to say, *really?* Then, he pushes against Vetris's other side. Grinning, I hoist Vetris's arm up higher and start to walk again, me on one side and a hellhound on the other. He weaves down the corridor, burping, singing, and praising my ass.

"So hot you can outdrink me," he slurs as we reach the doors to the chamber, and I nudge it open. "I have the best mate. You hear that, Soleil? I have the best mate ever!"

"Okay, time for bed," I say as he yells to everyone still awake and sober enough to understand him, which won't be many.

"Yes, bed, great idea." He wiggles his brows at me. "You can sit that pretty ass on my face, and I can show you my talents."

"Uh-huh, maybe some other time." I grin as I drag him over to the bed.

He pouts. "Why?"

"Because you are too drunk," I respond. "If you are a good boy and go to sleep, I will sit on your face in the morning."

"Deal," he slurs, leaning into me.

Grunting, I throw him onto the bed. He tumbles there, his wings spread as he watches me. "Come join me, mate," he slurs, reaching for me. Laughing, I dodge his hand, and he growls. “Angel, come cuddle,” he whines.

He’s fucking adorable—not that I would ever tell him that.

“Okay, mate,” I coo, knowing he’s ready to struggle to his feet to tug me down after him. I slide into our bed, and he flops over, yanking me against him and wrapping all limbs around me like a teddy bear.

“Love you, unicorn,” he slurs. “Such a pretty angel. Knew I would love you when you first kicked my ass. Was so hot.” His words don’t make much sense, but I smile anyway and kiss him softly.

“I love you too, Vetris.”

“Of course you do. I’m great and have an amazing penis,” he retorts, almost sounding offended.

“Of course, my prince.” I pat his chest, and he becomes quiet, tightening his hold on me.

Within a minute, he’s snoring. I can’t help but laugh as I close my eyes and soak in my mate’s warmth.

I am warm, content, and happy.

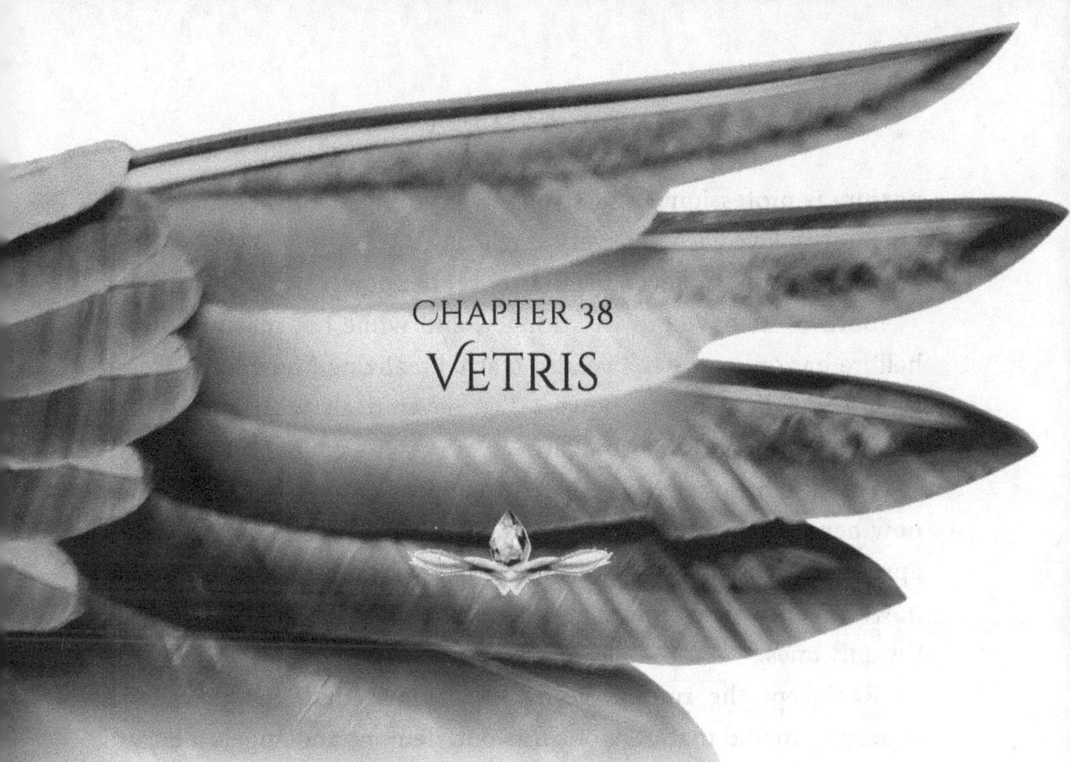

CHAPTER 38
VETRIS

My head hurts. Demons don't get hangovers, not really, but I'm damn close, especially after being woken up because we were apparently late. It was worth it, though, for the vision I have now. My mate glitters brightly beside me, her clothing a mixture between that of Soleil and Celestia. She spoke with one of our designers and had gotten some material from her home, and now, she wears clothing that fits both worlds.

Her outfit is reminiscent of her warrior clothing. Leather pants and a top wrap elegantly around her, with bits of hellfire-forged metal armor at her shoulders.

I want to take her back to Soleil and have my wicked way with her.

As if knowing where my thoughts are, she glances at me out of the corner of her eye and smiles.

"Later," she promises, the edges of her wings brushing mine in a way that makes me want to purr.

She's everything I've ever wanted.

The orange edges of her wings glitter in the sunlight, and her posture is professional and strong. Everything about her makes me fall more in love with her every single day.

And that doesn't even begin to cover her power.

Both of us have grown stronger, and while her mastery of my hellfire has only grown, I've also started realizing I now have access to some of her angelic powers I've never dealt with before, like inhaling glitter and absorbing it.

Small, dim runes have started to appear on my skin, hidden for now beneath my shirt, but I know one day they are going to be as apparent as the ones that run down her arms. We're becoming one powerful entity, a couple that no one can understand, and we aren't the only ones.

Rael kept the rumors going for so long that people weren't expecting to find mates. As it turns out, demons and angels alike are discovering their mates on the other side, and many have come forward, afraid of what's to come. We've been a steady comfort to them, showing that it's possible and that there's nothing to fear.

Roux has been great about that.

She's walked among my people and her own, offering advice and comfort when needed and helping when necessary.

She's strong, beautiful, and brilliant, and today, she's going to need every bit of that strength as we finally meet with the other seraphim.

We haven't heard much from them since the war. They have kept to their city, not mingling with demons like the other angels have. I've been waiting for them to declare war again, but instead, they answered our letter to have a meeting in the affirmative.

Then again, they watched Roux destroy one of them, so perhaps they answered out of fear.

We requested that the meeting be on neutral ground, but the seraphim have barely left their city since the war and requested we meet them in Celestia, in a holy hall that is usually reserved for the highest of the angels. Roux agreed because of the clear honor they intended, but something about it still rubs me the wrong way. I don't know why.

When we walk into the chamber in Celestia, however, they don't look afraid. They look reverent, and it's not directed at me.

It's directed at my mate.

"Roux," Josiah, the seraphim now sitting in the middle, coos. "We are pleased that you asked for our correspondence. You and your mate are welcome in our chamber anytime."

Roux shifts uncomfortably at this change, so I brush my wing against hers in comfort. She glances at me in gratitude, her wing settling heavily against mine.

"You haven't been seen in Soleil," she comments, getting straight to the point. "Is there a reason for that?"

Josiah shifts in his throne, and it's then I notice there's still an empty one where Rael used to sit. "Forgive us, but it's not something that comes easily for those of us who hardly remember a time when our two peoples weren't separated."

Another seraphim clears his throat. "We also were not certain we were welcome after Rael's treachery."

Roux tilts her head. "Were any of you complacent in his plans?"

I can feel her power, so I know they can as well. There's an audible shift in the room, and this time, I can smell true fear in the air.

"Of course not," Josiah murmurs. "We were mistaken in believing his lies, just as you were."

I doubt that. Soon, there will come a time where disagreements will happen. Even now, rumors of angels and demons protesting our new balanced world have surfaced, though none have yet made themselves known. For now, we'll continue to work on building a better world for all of our people, and when those who would fight it reveal themselves, we'll handle it.

"I only came to ask if the seraphim are willing to uphold the peace between us," Roux asks, reaching for my hand. "Soleil is prepared to sign a peace treaty. We have one here."

I produce the treaty I had drawn up and hand it to her, happy to be of help. This is her world. Though she's taken me through it and shown me where she lived, this place feels like I still don't belong. Only my connection to her keeps me from wanting to raze it to the ground.

"We are pleased by this turn of events," Josiah says, his eyes bright. A lower angel comes forward and takes the rolled treaty Roux holds out, bringing it to one of the other seraphim to read. "We also have a request for you."

"Oh?" Roux's hand tightens in mine, as if she suspects something great. These are people who were prepared to kill her for lies, and I know she no longer feels like she belongs here either. It pleases me that she wishes to remain in Soleil, even if I promise to fly with her through Celestia every chance she gets. In the end, we've managed to achieve something profound—a balance we didn't know our realm truly needed.

The green in the in-between is as bright as that in Celestia. Even Soleil has begun to sprout new life, and the sight makes something in me sing. Not even I have been alive long enough to remember a time when Soleil was lush and full of life.

"We find ourselves missing a seat on our seraphim council," Josiah begins. I tense at his words, understanding where this is going, and I'm not sure how my mate will take it. "We have come together and decided we would like you to accept that honor."

Roux doesn't tense like I do. Her gaze stays level on Josiah, her wings unmoving. I can see her mind working as she ponders her answer, and part of me fears that she'll accept and suddenly want better than what I can give. After all, she would have the power of a seraphim.

If she does, I will give up my claim to the throne and follow her here.

Wherever she is, I will follow.

She smiles. "Your honor is wasted on me, Josiah." The use of the other seraphim's name reveals all they need to know. She's more powerful than them and doesn't need a throne, and her use of his name makes it known. "No offense, but months ago, Celestia came after me for a crime I did not commit, and when you could not find me, you attacked Soleil in my name." Josiah tenses, but Roux isn't done. "The lives lost that day bear my name. I take that stain on my soul even though the seraphim responsible is now dead. Your offer does nothing but remind me of that treachery and what the other seven of you were willing to commit in your complacency."

Josiah blinks. "So you will not accept the seat of seraphim?"

Roux smiles and glances at me. "No, thank you. I already have my own throne." She looks back at Josiah. "And it's much prettier than that one."

Pride makes my chest swell. My wings drape over hers, supporting her in her decision. I would have supported her no matter what, but the way she addresses them reminds me just how strong my mate is.

She's changing our world, and she doesn't need some false title to do so.

"As you wish," Josiah replies, disappointment in his expression. He looks at the other seraphim who's reading the treaty. He nods and smiles gently. "We shall sign this peace treaty in good faith, and we hope that Soleil and Celestia will remain allies in the coming generations."

Roux barely inclines her head in a tiny show of respect. "We look forward to a new balance between our people." She smiles. "If you ever have need of me, send your correspondence to Soleil. That is where I shall reside."

They all sign the treaty before passing it back to us, and then we leave their chambers and the empty throne they dared to offer my mate after everything they did.

Because powerful allies win wars.

"I can't believe their audacity," she vents the moment we're free.

"Of course they'd want you," I murmur, pressing a kiss against her hair. "Look how magnificent you are."

She looks up at me brightly. "Can we go flying before we head back down? I'd like to visit Rosa and see how the demons living up here are getting on."

"Of course, my love. Anything for you."

We take to the skies, perfectly balanced, just as our world is slowly becoming. If someone were to come and try to throw chaos into this new world, then we'll meet them with sword and savagery together, just as we were always meant to.

CHAPTER 39
ROUX

The last few months have been crazy. Keeping the balance—which means settling squabbles between the princes and princess of Soleil who continue to start fights with angels, and the seraphim who like to test boundaries—has kept me and my mate busy, split between the two realms.

Our world is settling, regrowing, and rebirthing.

Angels live amongst demons in Soleil, and demons live amongst angels in Celestia.

Matings have taken place.

Some even choose to live on the surface with Abraxos, who has started his own little village there, even if it was unwillingly. Despite everything he has done and his obvious madness, I have a soft spot for the fallen angel. After all, he did everything for love, and I understand that.

I turn to the source of my love in pride.

He stands before his throne, awaiting the moment he will be crowned. Alongside the changes in our worlds, Soleil decided they needed some too. The crown will no longer randomly swap between the princes and princess. No, they voted—albeit a bloody, and long vote—that one will rule with the others acting as counsel. Some were against this at first, especially when Vetris was voted leader, but they soon realized it meant less responsibility and more time to get up to mischief, which they like. So yes, my mate is being crowned King of Soleil.

And I will be crowned as queen, which was decided by another vote, to oversee both worlds.

A king needs a queen, and a queen needs her king.

I go to mine now. My long blue dress trails behind me, fashioned after the stars with golden moons and celestial bodies sewn into the corseted bodice and train. The end is singed as if fire has touched it, and a golden necklace, a gift from my mate, hangs between my breasts—a two-part locket, one the sun, and the other the moon.

Just like us.

Night and day.

He holds out his hand for me, his eyes sparkling with love and lust as he watches me walk toward him. The hall is filled with both angels and demons, all trying to get a look. My hellhounds trot proudly around me, growling and snapping at anyone who gets too close. Gerkun fans out my train, throwing black flowers of hellfire in my wake.

After all, this is not just a crowning, but a wedding.

Our wedding.

Vetris's black pants have flames crawling across them, and his chest is bare except for a tattoo that matches my locket. A fur-trimmed cape lines his shoulders, and his crown sits atop his head. Next to his throne is a matching one—gold to his black—waiting for its queen.

When I reach him, I place my hand in his, and despite tradition, he quickly tugs me closer and kisses me hard, making me whimper. When his voice comes, it's soft and low, just for us. "You are magnificent, mate."

"So are you." I trace his tattoo and smile up at him. "Now let's get married so we can enjoy our honeymoon."

That gets him moving quickly, and the crowd laughs at our antics.

Most of the ceremony is a blur. I'm too focused on my mate, even as we kneel and are crowned. My crown is a gold celestial design that my mate chose, and when it settles upon my head, the hellfire that lives within me crawls across my skin and lights it up like his. The crowd gasps, but my mate simply smiles as if he knew it would happen.

After that, we are told to stand and kiss, and then it is done. We are mated, married, and coronated.

The room erupts in chaotic celebration. I smile at my people, pleased to have come so far, but then my mate tugs me down onto my throne and sits upon his. Our hands remain clasped across the arms, and my eyes stray to his, taking in the sight of the demon I love.

"Are you ready for this every day?" he teases.

"Are you ready for forever?" I retort.

"With you, unicorn? Without a doubt. I was waiting for you my whole life. I just didn't know it. Now, let's be the best fucking king and queen they have ever seen." He winks as a song begins, taken up by the crowd. "Starting with getting my queen in the spirit and then fucking her royal pussy raw later for all of our kingdom to hear."

"Such a charmer," I joke, even as fire races through me.

"You love it." He grins.

"No, I love you," I reply, leaning in to kiss him.

And so there, in the middle of Soleil, an angel and a demon embrace as equals, lovers, and rulers.

Our world rejoices with us, and peace is restored at last.

EPILOGUE

ROUX

A YEAR LATER...

The wind soars under my wings, lifting me higher and higher, and I close my eyes in bliss as I spread them to hover midair. Power and strength radiate through me until a voice calls out.

"Are you getting slow in your old age, mate?"

Rolling my eyes, I focus on Vetris, who's flying circles below me. With a teasing wink, he begins to dive. I follow after him with a laugh, tucking in my wings to catch up. We glide past Celestia, where those milling about wave, and I wave back, happy to see them content and living full lives. I know many of them personally, and when I see Rosa, I can't help but smile. It took many moons, but the last seraphim seat was finally filled by her. She is a worthy angel, one with a demon mate who worships the ground she walks on. She makes sure the others stay in line and helps keep an eye on Celestia while my mate and I reside within Soleil, building our home and world.

Vetris's laughter floats on the air, and I tuck my wings in tighter, intent on catching him this time. I draw closer and closer, and everything else fades away. As I'm about to hit him, he turns with his arms wide to catch me, just like he always does.

We crash together, all limbs, wings, and laughter, and tumble to the ground below, landing in a field of flowers.

I giggle as he rains kisses along my brow. All around us, greenery grows as far as the eye can see with food, foliage, flowers, and even a forest. Our world is slowly healing. There are still some scars upon this realm that will never heal, but it is a daily reminder of all we have suffered to get here.

In the distance, I hear Abraxos teaching angels and demons alike how to fight, forage, and live together in peace. His lands here have grown in the last year, and more often than not, we spend the night. Despite everything, he's a good friend, and he's slowly warming up to Vetris... very slowly.

"My beautiful unicorn."

"Don't you forget it, princess," I tease.

"That's *King* Princess to you," he retorts, lying back. His wings are spread around him, and his arms pillow his head as his eyes sparkle with mischief. After all, my mate is still a demon. "And what will you do now that you have caught me, my queen?"

Leaning down, I bite his plump lower lip, making him moan. "Have my wicked way with you, of course," I purr as I straddle his waist. The sun heats our skin, and the ground below welcomes us as we flow into one another.

We are entities of both worlds, a love that should never have been.

A king of hell.

A queen of the skies.

We are mates, even as he burns me and I free him.

I don't know what the future holds, but as I stare down at the love of my life, I know that with him at my side, we can handle anything that comes our way.

ABOUT K.A. KNIGHT

K.A Knight is an international bestselling indie author trying to get all of the stories and characters out of her head, writing the monsters that you love to hate. She loves reading and devours every book she can get her hands on, and she also has a worrying caffeine addiction.

She leads her double life in a sleepy English town, where she spends her days writing like a crazy person.

Read more at K.A Knight's website or join her Facebook Reader Group.
Sign up for exclusive content and my newsletter here
http://eepurl.com/drLLoj

About Kendra Moreno

Kendra Moreno is secretly a spy but when she's not dealing in secrets and espionage, you can find her writing her latest adventure. She lives in Texas where the summer days will make you melt, and southern charm comes free with every meal. She's a recovering Road Rager (kind of) and slowly overcoming her Star Wars addiction (nope!), and she definitely didn't pass on her addiction to her son (she did). She has one hellhound named Mayhem who got tired of guarding the Gates of Hell and now guards her home against monsters. She's a geek, a mother, a scuba diver, a tyrannosaurus rex, and a wordsmith who sometimes switches out her pen for a sword.

If you see Kendra on the streets, don't worry: you can distract her with talks about Kylo Ren or Loki.
#LokiLives #BringBackBenSolo

To find out more about Kendra, you can check her out on her website or join her
Facebook group, Kendra's World of Wonder.
Sign up for Kendra's Newsletter:
https://mailchi.mp/feb46d2b29ad/babbleandquill

facebook.com/AuthorKendraMoreno

twitter.com/KendramorenoA

instagram.com/kendramorenoauthor

bookbub.com/authors/kendra-moreno

Also by K.A. Knight

THEIR CHAMPION SERIES *Dystopian RH*

The Wasteland

The Summit

The Cities

The Nations

Their Champion Coloring Book

Their Champion - the omnibus

The Forgotten

The Lost

The Damned

Their Champion Companion - the omnibus

DAWNBREAKER SERIES *SCI FI RH*

Voyage to Ayama

Dreaming of Ayama

THE LOST COVEN SERIES *PNR RH*

Aurora's Coven

Aurora's Betrayal

HER MONSTERS SERIES *PNR RH*

Rage

Hate

THE FALLEN GODS SERIES *PNR*

Pretty Painful

Pretty Bloody

Pretty Stormy

Pretty Wild

Pretty Hot

Pretty Faces

Pretty Spelled

Fallen Gods - the omnibus 1

Fallen Gods - the omnibus 2

FORBIDDEN READS *(STANDALONES)* *CONTEMPORARY*

Daddy's Angel

Stepbrothers' Darling

PRETTY LIARS *CONTEMPORARY RH*

Unstoppable

Book 2 coming soon..

FORGOTTEN CITY *PNR RH*

Monstrous Lies

Monstrous Truths

Monstrous Ends

STANDALONES

IN DEN OF VIPERS' UNIVERSE - CONTEMPORARY

Scarlett Limerence

Nadia's Salvation

Alena's Revenge

Den of Vipers

Gangsters and Guns (Co-Write with Loxley Savage)

CONTEMPORARY

The Standby

Diver's Heart

SCI FI RH

Crown of Stars

AUDIOBOOKS

The Wasteland

The Summit

Rage

Hate

Den of Vipers *(From Podium Audio)*

Gangsters and Guns *(From Podium Audio)*

Daddy's Angel *(From Podium Audio)*

Stepbrothers' Darling *(From Podium Audio)*

Blade of Iris *(From Podium Audio)*

Deadly Affair *(From Podium Audio)*

Stolen Trophy *(From Podium Audio)*

Crown of Stars *(From Podium Audio)*

SHARED WORLD PROJECTS

Blade of Iris - Mafia Wars *CONTEMPORARY*

CO-AUTHOR PROJECTS - *Erin O'Kane*

HER FREAKS SERIES *PNR Dystopian RH*

Circus Save Me

Taming The Ringmaster

Walking the Tightrope

Her Freaks Series - the omnibus

STANDALONES

PNR RH

The Hero Complex

Collection of Short Stories

Dark Temptations (contains One Night Only and Circus Saves Christmas)

THE WILD BOYS SERIES *CONTEMPORARY*

The Wild Interview

The Wild Tour

The Wild Finale

The Wild Boys - the omnibus

CO-AUTHOR PROJECTS - *Ivy Fox*

Deadly Love Series *CONTEMPORARY*

Deadly Affair

Deadly Match

Deadly Encounter

CO-AUTHOR PROJECTS - *Kendra Moreno*

STANDALONES

CONTEMPORARY

Stolen Trophy

PNR RH

Fractured Shadows

Burn Me

CO-AUTHOR PROJECTS - *Loxley Savage*

THE FORSAKEN SERIES *SCI FI RH*

Capturing Carmen

Stealing Shiloh

Harboring Harlow

STANDALONES

Gangsters and Guns - IN DEN OF VIPERS' UNIVERSE

OTHER CO-WRITES

Shipwreck Souls *(with Kendra Moreno & Poppy Woods)*

The Horror Emporium *(with Kendra Moreno & Poppy Woods)*

Also by Kendra

Sons Of Wonderland

Book 1 - Mad as a Hatter

Book 2 - Late as a Rabbit

Book 3 - Feral as a Cat

Companion novel - Cruel as a Queen

Daughters Of Neverland

Book 1 - Vicious as a Darling

Book 2 - Fierce As A Tiger Lily

Book 3 - Wicked As A Pixie

Companion Novel - Monstrous As A Croc

The Heirs Of Oz

Book 1 - Heartless as a Tin Man

Book 2 - Empty as a Scarecrow

Book 3 - Cowardly as a Lion

Companion Novel - Vengeful as a Beauty

The Lords of Grimm

Book 1 - Cunning as a Trickster

Book 2 - Bitter as a Captain

Book 3 - Twisted as a Princess

Companion Novel - Hateful as a Sister

The Keepers of Enchantment

Book 1 - Charming as a Killer

Prey Island

Book 1 - Prey Island

Book 2 - Predator Point

Clockwork Almanac

Book 1 - Clockwork Butterfly

Book 2 - Clockwork Octopus

The Valhalla Mechanism

Book 1 - Gears of Mischief

Book 2 - Gears of Thunder

Book 3 - Gears of Ragnarök

Race Games

Book 1 - Blood and Honey

Book 2 - Teeth and Wings

Book 3 - Jewels and Feathers

Book 3 - Fur and Claws

Stand-alones

Treble Maker

Pharaoh-mones

CO-WRITES

with K.A Knight

Stolen Trophy

Fractured Shadows

Burn Me

with K.A Knight and Poppy Woods

Shipwreck Souls

The Horror Emporium

with Poppy Woods

The Blooming Courts

Book 1 - Resurrect

Book 2 - Sprout

Book 3 - Flourish

Book 4 - Emerge

Book 5 - Blossom

The Dinoverse

(Shared universe with Poppy Woods)

Book 1 – Dances with Raptors by Poppy Woods

Book 2 – Rexes & Robbers by Kendra Moreno

Head Case: A Dark Twist on a Classic

www.ingramcontent.com/pod-product-compliance
Lightning Source LLC
Chambersburg PA
CBHW010448310726
48979CB00018B/2858/J